The Incredible
Cat Caper

The Incredible Cat Caper

Kelley Roos and
Stephen Roos

ILLUSTRATED BY
KATHERINE COVILLE

DELACORTE PRESS / NEW YORK

Published by
Delacorte Press
1 Dag Hammarskjold Plaza
New York, N.Y. 10017

MANUFACTURED IN THE UNITED STATES OF AMERICA
FIRST PRINTING
Library of Congress Cataloging in Publication Data
Roos, Kelley.
    The incredible cat caper.
    Summary: A move to a condominium where no pets are allowed
forces twelve-year-old Jessie to hide her cat, Simba, in her room.
    1. Children's stories, American. [1. Cats—Fiction.
2. Condominium (Housing)—Fiction. 3. Burglary—Fiction. 4. Mystery
and detective stories] I. Roos, Stephen. II. Coville, Katherine, ill.
III. Title.
PZ7.R6747In 1985   [Fic]
ISBN 0-385-29408-5
Library of Congress Catalog Card Number: 85–1626

for Carol Roos Bell

Chapter 1

9:46 P.M., THURSDAY

The night was perfect, absolutely perfect, the sort of night most people only dream about. Palm trees swayed in the tropical breezes and waves sent up a gentle roar as they crashed along the beach. The temperature was perfect too. Low seventies. Tonight you didn't need a sweater. What could be more perfect than that?

A moon, some might say. And stars. Tonight there was no moon and the stars were few and far between. Tonight the skies were dark, pitch black almost. A lot of people like their nights filled with light. But for the sinister figure standing at the top of the tower of the condominium, the dark night was absolutely perfect.

Turning its gaze from the skies to a balcony two flights below, the figure grasped the railing at the edge of the roof and swung over it.

Whoooooosh! In one thrilling swoop, the figure was falling through the air. A moment later, its hands caught the railing on a terrace. Whoooooosh! It swung to another balcony until it landed on the terrace of apartment 12G, the target for tonight.

Without pausing to catch its breath, the figure crossed the terrace to the sliding door. As expected, the door was unlocked. It slid the door open and tiptoed into the apartment as quickly and as lightly as a cat. The night's work had only just begun. There wasn't a second to lose.

The cat burglar was striking again!

Chapter 2

2:11 P.M., SUNDAY

There was nothing unusual about two of the girls waiting at the corner for the traffic light to change. It was the third girl, the tall one in the middle with the long blond hair that curled just above her shoulders, who looked odd. Even if you thought she was pretty, and just about everyone who saw her did, you still would have thought she looked very definitely odd.

"Look, Mommy!" a little boy shouted as the light changed and the three girls passed by in the middle of the street. "That girl! She's wearing a cat!"

The tall blond girl and her two friends laughed, but they didn't say anything. They knew that the cat, whose name was Simba, was the descendant of Siamese warrior cats who long ago had ridden into battle on their masters' shoulders to protect them from the enemy.

3

Even though there weren't any enemies in Toronto, Simba liked riding on the tall girl's shoulder. The tall girl, whose name was Jessica, liked to think her cat was keeping up the family tradition of Siamese cats.

"It's not the first time you and Simba stopped traffic," said Molly, who was walking on one side of Jessica.

"But I guess it's the last," said Frieda, the girl on the other side. All of a sudden Frieda wanted to bite her tongue. "I didn't mean that," she stammered. "I didn't mean to make you feel any worse than you already do."

"It's okay," Jessie said, even though she didn't feel the slightest bit okay. "Come on. We've got one last piece of business to take care of."

The three girls kept walking along the icy pavement to Adele's house. That was where the Hijinx Club had held its meetings for the past four years. It was probably the only club in the world whose members were all officers. Simba had a title too. She was the club's official mascot.

Before the girls could ring the doorbell, Adele's mother opened the door. She was dressed in a fur coat.

"Adele's in her room," Mrs. Cole said. "She's waiting for you. I'm afraid I've got to run."

"Good-bye, Mrs. Cole," Jessie said.

"Good-bye, dear," Mrs. Cole said as she gave

Jessie a hug. "And don't worry about Simba. We'll take good care of her."

"I know you will," Jessie said. "Thank you, Mrs. Cole."

Mrs. Cole hurried off and the three girls went inside. When they reached the upstairs, they found Adele lying on her bed, listening to the radio. She held a finger to her lips so that none of them would say anything.

"Starting late this afternoon," the radio announcer was saying, "seven to nine inches of snow are predicted for Toronto, more in the suburbs. It looks like we're in for another record-breaking cold front too. Oh, you lucky people who are southbound for sunny Florida!"

Jessie's groan was so loud that it frightened Simba. She leaped from Jessie's shoulder and looked back to see what was wrong up there. Adele snapped off the radio.

"What is it, Jessie?" Adele asked. "What he said about Florida?"

"I guess I was hoping the snow would come earlier," she said. "In time to shut down the airport."

"But it's warm in Florida," Frieda said.

"And it's sunny," Molly said.

"It can't be all bad," Adele said. "Your mother and your new father are there."

5

"If you guys don't stop trying to cheer me up, I'm going to cry," Jessie said.

"You're sure to meet nice people there," Frieda said, trying, in spite of what Jessie had said, to look on the bright side.

"Not at the Tudor Towers, I won't," Jessie said. "All the people who live in the condo are horrible."

"How can you be so sure?" Molly asked.

"Because they don't allow pets," Jessie said. "That's how I know."

Simba, whose head had been resting on Jessie's right foot, jumped into Jessie's lap. Although it hardly seemed possible, it was as though Simba had understood what Jessie was saying.

"Are you mad at your new father?" Molly asked.

"I don't know," Jessie said slowly. "I was at first. For not reading the fine print. And David's a lawyer too. I'm not mad at him anymore, I guess. C'mon. Let's get the meeting over with. I've got a plane to catch."

"How soon?" Frieda asked.

"My aunt's picking me up at three," Jessie said.

"So let's get going," Adele said sadly. "I don't want to, but I hereby call the last and final meeting of the Hijinx Club to order."

6

"What do you mean 'last and final' meeting?" Jessie asked. "You're going to keep the club together, aren't you?"

"Without you, Jessie?" Adele asked. "How could we?"

Jessie looked at Molly and Frieda. They were nodding their heads.

"You're our leader," Frieda said.

"You founded us," Molly cried.

"Okay, that's true, but—"

"No buts," Adele said. Just when it looked like she was about to cry, she started to giggle instead. Jessie and Molly and Frieda couldn't believe it.

"What's so funny?" Molly asked.

"I was thinking about our first hijinx," Adele said. "Remember when Jessie had us set the alarm clocks in the store?"

"So they all went off at once," Frieda said, giggling too now.

"Everybody got practically hysterical and ran out of the store," Molly said. She was laughing so hard she had to gasp for breath.

"And the Watkins twins wet their pants," Jessie said. For the first time in days, she was laughing along with the others. "How about the time we set all the mousetraps over at Ace Hardware?"

7

"It was hilarious," Frieda said. "It was the best."

"No, the time Jessie pretended to be a midget," Molly said. "That was the best."

Frieda and Molly and Adele were all talking at once.

"At the movies," Molly said. "You got insulted when the cashier gave you a kid's half-price ticket. You started yelling that you were a thirty-five-year-old midget."

"You said that Molly was your daughter," Frieda said.

"And the cashier got mad and called in the manager," Adele said.

"And he believed you," Molly said. "He made the cashier apologize to you."

"And he let both of us in for free," Frieda said.

Then all four girls were quiet, thinking about all the fun they would never have because Jessie was moving to Florida.

"Hey," Adele said. "I've got an idea! Jessie, it would be the greatest hijinx of your career! And it would solve everything for you!"

"What?" Jessie said. "Tell me!"

"Take Simba with you," Adele said.

"With me . . . to Florida?"

"Yes. Sneak her onto the plane with you. Hide her in a shopping bag!"

8

"That's smuggling," Jessie said. "It's an international crime."

"Yes," Frieda said excitedly. "But think of it as an international hijinx."

"But they don't allow pets in the condo," Jessie said. "Mom and David won't let me keep her."

"Hide her in your room," Frieda said.

"Without them knowing? How am I going to pull that one off?"

"You'll think of something," Molly said. "You always have, Jessie."

"There's nothing I'd like more than to keep Simba with me," Jessie said. "But I don't know how I could do it all by myself."

"You won't be alone," Molly said. "You'll have Simba with you."

"Well, yes, but . . ."

"She'll help out," Adele said. "She's incredibly intelligent."

"Not to mention incredibly brave and incredibly beautiful," Molly added.

"Face it, Jessie," Frieda said. "Simba is one incredible cat. Together the two of you can do anything."

Simba stood up on Jessie's lap, put a front paw on each of her shoulders, and rubbed her face against Jessie's.

9

"You're outvoted," Molly said. "It's four to one. You're taking Simba to Florida."

"Adele, get a shopping bag," Frieda said.

"Yes, and I'll get those tranquilizers the vet gave us for our cat," Adele said. "One of them will keep Simba quiet for hours."

"What happens when your mother realizes that Simba's not here?" Jessie asked.

"I'll tell her that Simba's at Molly's or Frieda's," Adele said. "No one will ever know except the four of us."

"And Simba won't tell," Molly said. "She's one cat who knows how to keep a secret."

As the girls rushed around getting Simba ready, Jessie heard her aunt honk the horn three times. "It's time for me to leave," she said. Then she corrected herself. "It's time for Simba and me to leave, I mean."

All at once the girls were laughing and hugging and crying and giving Jessie farewell presents. Even if it was wrong to smuggle a cat across international borders, Jessie knew she was doing the right thing. And from the way Simba swallowed the tranquilizer without complaining and then jumped into the shopping bag, it seemed she agreed.

The girls were right, Jessie thought. Simba was one incredible cat.

Chapter 3

3:05 P.M., SUNDAY

The ride to the airport had gone off without a hitch. Aunt Bea parked the car and walked with Jessie as far as the ticket counter. Jessie checked her suitcase through to Miami, but she held on to the shopping bag. Simba was sound asleep. On top of Simba was a bathing suit for Jessie from Adele, a beach towel from Frieda, and a beach robe from Molly. Simba, Jessie thought, could not have been better hidden in a haystack.

"Well, good-bye, my dear," Aunt Bea said in her important, executive voice. "Try to be a good girl. None of your tricks on the plane or on David. And give your mother and David my love."

"Thanks for everything," Jessie said.

"Bless you, dear girl," Aunt Bea said.

Aunt Bea strode away without kissing her good-bye. Jessie wished she had. Suddenly she

THE INCREDIBLE CAT CAPER

felt all alone. If only Simba weren't asleep, it would have been better. But that would have been impossible, of course. Clutching the shopping bag to her chest, she found gate 17.

"You carrying that bag onto the plane?" the gate attendant asked her.

"My good man," Jessie said, using Aunt Bea's deep, executive voice, "have you any objections?"

"Hey, kid," the attendant said, "where did you get a voice like that, a kid like you?"

"I'm not a kid, thank you," Jessie said in Aunt Bea's voice. "I am a midget, aged thirty-five."

"Okay," the attendant laughed. "But I've got to put that bag through the electronic detector."

"My good man," Jessie said, "are you accusing me of packing a rod?"

"Sorry, Mrs. Midget," he said. "It's the rules."

He held out a hand for the shopping bag. Jessie hesitated, but she knew she had no choice. She hadn't thought about electronic detectors at airports. What if the metal clips on Simba's plastic collar were enough to set off the alarm? What if Simba woke up and gave away the whole plan? What if the attendant could see Simba's skeleton on the little screen at the side of the detector?

Jessie held her breath and waited for the alarms to ring and the Royal Mounted Police to arrive to take her and Simba off to jail.

"Your bag, miss," the attendant said.

"Huh?"

"Here's your shopping bag," he said, holding it out for her. "Is your husband a midget too?"

"No, he's a giant," Jessie said.

Trying hard to hide the wave of relief that was flooding her, Jessie took the bag and walked through the gate. She peeked in the bag. One motionless paw was resting on top of the beach robe. Some haystack, Jessie thought. With her free hand, she covered the paw.

Her seat on the plane was by the window. The stewardess took her winter coat and packed it in the compartment above the center aisle.

"Would you like me to put your bag there too?" she asked.

"No, thanks," Jessie said quickly. "I'll keep it with me."

"Okay," the stewardess said. "But put it under the seat in front of you during the takeoff and the landing."

"Is that a rule?"

"Oh, yes," the stewardess said. "It's for your safety."

More rules, Jessie thought, and shook her head. She set the bag on the floor in front of her. Simba was still fast asleep. Atta girl, Simba.

Jessie buckled her seat belt and tried to make herself comfortable. But not too comfortable.

15

She had a lot of planning to do. How was she going to keep Simba safely hidden on the way from the airport to the Tudor Towers in Christmas Cove? And then how was she going to hide Simba from her mother and David when they reached the apartment? After a few minutes she realized she wasn't going to be able to cross those bridges until she came to them. Meanwhile, at least, no one had been assigned to the two seats beside her. That was a break. The last thing she needed was a nosy neighbor or two.

"Hello there, little girl," said a voice almost on top of her. "It looks like we're going to be seatmates."

Jessie looked up. A woman with the brightest red hair she had ever seen was pointing at the aisle seat. Although the seat between them was still empty, the lady was dangerously close.

Quickly, before the lady sat down, Jessie said, "Hey, wait a minute! You sure that's your seat?"

"Why, yes." She looked at her ticket, checking it out. "Yes, 18A."

"Wait! That seat's no good!"

"Really?"

"I tried it," Jessie said. "It's lumpy."

"Lumpy?"

"I'll say! Boy, is it ever lumpy!"

"Well," the lady said. "I'll see for myself."

She plunked herself down into the seat and

squirmed her bottom around, thoroughly testing it. "Why, it's a lovely seat!" She smiled at Jessica. "I think, my dear, that maybe it's you that's lumpy."

"I guess so," Jessie said. "I never noticed before."

"Traveling all by yourself?"

"No," Jessie said, flustered by the lady being so close to Simba. "I mean yes, but please don't worry about me."

"Of course not. You look perfectly capable."

The sound system crackled and the captain welcomed them aboard. Then the head stewardess took over with the safety instructions. Jessie was glad for the interruption. If she had to have a "seatmate," she didn't want her to get too matey. What could she do to stop that? Think fast, she told herself. Be as capable as the lady said she looked. Jessie yawned. She would pretend to be asleep. That would keep the lady from talking to her. First, she anchored the shopping bag with her feet. Then she yawned another big yawn and closed her eyes. With all her might she pretended to be asleep.

The next thing she knew someone was tapping her on the shoulder. She heard the lady's voice practically in her ear. "I'm sure, my dear, you would rather at your age have a Coke than a nap."

17

Jessie opened her eyes, pulled herself together, and looked out the window. "We're in the air already!"

"My, yes. For more than an hour now."

More than an hour, Jessie thought. That meant she wasn't in Canada anymore. The Mounties couldn't get her now. She was in the United States, or over it. She reminded herself not to pretend to go to sleep again. She wasn't good at it.

"Cal or no-cal," the stewardess said. She was standing in the aisle with a cartload of cans, bottles, plastic cups, and ice.

"Either one, thanks."

"One no-cal Coke," the stewardess said, "coming up."

As she poured the Coke into one of the plastic cups, Jessie felt the shopping bag stir between her feet. She prayed that Simba was only rolling over in her sleep.

The stewardess handed the Coke to the redheaded lady and the redheaded lady handed it plus a smile to Jessie. Jessie tried to return the smile, but it was the worst smile she had ever smiled. Simba, she was thinking, please still be asleep. Please.

"Would you like some peanuts?" the stewardess asked.

"No, thanks," Jessie said. "Not now."

All she wanted in the whole wide world was for Simba to quiet down. But just the opposite was happening. Simba was still moving around in her shopping bag. Then, worse than that, she started making noises. Strange noises. Jessie couldn't tell how Simba could be making them. But they were coming out of the bag and Simba was the only thing in there that could be making them.

The redheaded lady was busy blowing her nose so the stewardess leaned across to give Jessie the peanuts.

"I thought you might change your mind," she said. Then she said, "What's that noise?"

"Noise?" Jessie said, trying to drown out the noise. "What noise?"

"I'm hearing something," the stewardess said firmly. "And it's coming from around here. I better report it to the captain."

Only a miracle can save me now, Jessie thought. Please, someone, send me one. But the stewardess straightened up and turned to report Simba's noise to the captain. It was too late.

"Wait, miss," the lady said. "It's me, the noise."

"You?" the stewardess said dubiously.

"I'm afraid so. This nasty cold of mine, this wheezing," the lady said. "I'm taking it to Florida to be cured." Now she was wheezing so well

19

that Simba's noise was drowned out. "There's no need to report my cold to the captain, is there?"

The stewardess laughed. "Not at all," she laughed. "Sorry to have alarmed the two of you."

"But she didn't, did she, my dear?"

"Not, not a bit," Jessie lied happily.

"Well, no harm done. Good luck in Florida with your cold," the stewardess said as she pushed her cart to the next row of seats.

Jessie turned her head and took a good look at the lady. She wasn't wheezing anymore. And why was she smiling at her?

"We wouldn't want, would we," she said, "to let the cat out of the bag?"

"You knew!"

"While you were asleep, your bag made some noises and I sneaked a look into it. I'm a cat lover myself. I wouldn't want a cat of mine to travel in a cage all alone in the luggage compartment."

"I'll remember to thank you every day for the rest of my life," Jessie said. "So will Simba. That's my cat—Simba."

"A lovely name," the lady said. "Simba seems to have quieted down, but just in case, if you have any pacifying pills . . ."

"I'll give her one more," Jessie said.

"Do that," the lady said. "And it will cure my cold too."

She stood up, shielding Jessie so that nobody

could see her give Simba the pill. When she was finished with Simba and Simba was quieting down some more, the lady sat down.

"Thanks again," Jessie said.

"No more thanks. Any true cat lover would do the same. Fortunately the world is full of cat lovers."

"Florida too?" Jessie asked.

"Yes, Florida too. Wherever there are civilized people."

Jessie decided to spare the lady the bad news that there was at least one condo in Florida that was chock full of uncivilized people who were very anticat.

"What if the captain had found Simba," Jessie said. "I could be on my way to jail for cat smuggling!"

The lady laughed as though she didn't believe that, but she didn't say so. Instead she said, "The pill should get you both safely to Florida. Your life in crime will soon be over."

Jessie nodded but not very sincerely. Her life in crime, she thought, was only just beginning.

Chapter 4

5:48 A.M., MONDAY

When Jessie woke the next morning, she didn't know where she was. She saw Simba sleeping on the other pillow beside hers. That didn't help any. That was where Simba had slept ever since she was a kitten. Then Jessie saw the shopping bag on a chair across the room. Now she knew where she and Simba were. They were in Florida. Christmas Cove. The Tudor Towers condominium, where pets, even cats, were not permitted.

Her mother and David had met her at the airport. Everything had gone smoothly. No problems. Simba had still been asleep when they had arrived at the Tudor Towers the night before and Jessie had kept her hidden behind the shower curtain in her own private bathroom until she and her mother and David had said goodnight. Then Jessie had let Simba out into her own private bedroom and both of them had fallen asleep.

Now Simba was awake. She stood up on her pillow and made a noise that meant she was hungry. No wonder, Jessie thought. Except for some water, Simba hadn't had anything to eat since yesterday morning. Jessie looked at her clock. It wasn't six yet. Her mother and David would still be asleep. Jessie got some milk from the fridge. Simba enjoyed it thoroughly.

An hour later there was a knock on Jessie's door.

"Don't come in!" Jessie yelled.

Her mother laughed. "I won't, darling. I promise. Breakfast on the terrace in ten minutes."

"Okay. Thanks."

When Jessie came out onto the terrace, she walked as though she were in a trance. She looked blankly at her mother and at David. In a small, thin voice, she said, "Oh, sorry. I must have the wrong terrace."

"What, Jessie?" her mother asked.

"Who's Jessie?" Jessie asked. "Who are you? I've never seen either one of you before." She put her fingers on her forehead. "I'm sorry. It's not your fault. I seem to have amnesia something awful."

24

"Jessica!" her mother said sternly. "None of your . . ."

David interrupted her. "Wait. This might be serious. Jessie, did you get hit on the head?"

"I don't remember, but I must have. I can't remember anything. If you know who I am, please tell me."

"You mean who you really are?" David asked.

"Sure. My family must be worried sick about me."

"You don't remember the explosion?" David asked.

"What explosion?"

"Just before the ship sank, of course."

"There was a shipwreck?"

Then Jessie realized what was happening. First she had hijinxed David. Now he was hijinxing her back. Jessie wished Simba were out on the terrace enjoying herself too. Then everything would be superperfect.

"How did I wind up with you?"

"When I was deep-sea fishing, I caught you by mistake."

"What's going to happen to me now?" Jessie asked.

"We have to throw you back in the ocean," David said. "You're too small. As soon as you finish your corn flakes, it's back to the deep blue."

25

"Watch out for sharks, dear," her mother said. "We wouldn't want your family to worry about you."

"But you're my family," Jessie said. "You can't throw me to the sharks. I've got to start school this morning."

"Hijinxed you!" her mother said, laughing.

"And we won," David said. He was laughing too.

"It's not fair," Jessie said. "I was trying to hijinx the two of you!"

"Serves you right," her mother said. "I thought you were going to control your hijinx when you came to Christmas Cove."

"Sometimes I just can't help myself, Mom," Jessie said. "Besides, Aunt Bea gave me the idea. She told me not to do it to David."

David laughed some more.

"Have your breakfast, darling," her mother said. "You mustn't be late for school the first day."

Jessie had almost forgotten about school. How could she think up a way to keep her mother and David from finding Simba while she was out of the apartment? When the solution came to her, she had to credit her quick-wittedness to her Hijinx Club training, even if the solution was only temporary.

"Mom, David," she said. "I have a surprise for you!"

"Shall we guess which hand?" her mother asked.

"It's a big surprise," Jessie said. "It's too big for hands. It's a wedding present."

"How lovely," her mother said. "Did you bring it all the way from Toronto?"

"Yes and no," Jessie said. "I mean I brought part of it but it's going to take two weeks to get it ready."

"We're going to have to wait two long weeks?" David asked.

"It'll be worth it," Jessie said. "I'm going to make it myself. In my room. So you'll have to promise me something. Will you? Both of you?"

"I promise to make you a promise," David said.

"Mom?"

"I'd like to know what it is first . . . but all right. What is it?"

"Promise me starting this minute," Jessie said. "Neither of you will go into my room for two whole weeks."

"Starting this minute?" her mother asked. "You couldn't have begun to make it already. You just arrived last night."

"I know that," Jessie said. "But the part I

27

brought—if you see it, it'll spoil everything. Promise? Cross your hearts and hope to die?"

Crossing their hearts and hoping to die, her mother and David promised.

"Can I drop you off at school?" David asked. "It's on my way, Jessie."

"No, thanks," she answered. "I'm pretty sure I remember everything from last month when I came down and Mom got me registered."

While David kissed Jessie and her mother good-bye, picked up his briefcase, and left the apartment, Jessie thought of how much she liked the Tudor Towers the first time she had seen it and how much she had looked forward to living there, even though it meant leaving Toronto. But that was before David had read the fine print in the lease and discovered that cats were outlawed in the condo.

"I'm sorry about Simba not being here with you, Jess," her mother said. It was eerie, almost as though her mother was reading her mind. "David is too. We both feel rotten about it."

"It's okay," Jessie said, a little guiltily. "I don't want you to worry about Simba or me."

"I told David how much Simba means to you, about how she was the last present Dad gave you before he died," her mother said. "He tried hard to convince Mr. Rodriguez to let Simba into the condo."

"Who's Mr. Rodriguez?" Jessie asked.

"He's the manager of the Tudor Towers," her mother explained. "He's a very nice man, Jess, but he couldn't change the rules just for us."

"He wouldn't even bend them a little?" Jessie asked. "Even for Simba?"

"David wouldn't ask anyone to bend the rules," her mother said. "Lawyers don't do that, and David's a very good lawyer."

Jessie nodded. She knew David was a good lawyer. He was also a very successful one. He had practiced law in Christmas Cove for almost fifteen years and everyone in town who knew him admired him.

"David wants both of us to be happy here," her mother said. "He'd do practically anything for us."

"You're happy, aren't you, Mom?" Jessie asked. "You look happy."

"I feel every bit as happy as I look," her mother said. "And I owe it to you and to David, honey. It looks like I've lucked out in the husband and daughter departments."

"Well, I guess it's not every mother who gets a daughter who's beautiful, brilliant, and has a terrific personality," Jessie admitted. "And David's pretty terrific too, even if he does go out of his way to obey the law too much."

29

"Jess," her mother said, "you don't mean that."

"Okay," she said. "I mean everyone should obey all the laws all the time. Except this time maybe."

"David did what he could," her mother said. "And you know that Simba's in fine hands."

"She couldn't be in finer hands, as a matter of fact," Jessie said. "I know that."

"It's time for my beautiful, brilliant, and all-around terrific daughter to be on her way," Mrs. Bradley said. She kissed Jessica on the cheek. "Are you a little anxious about your first day at a new school, dear?"

"I've been so busy that I haven't had enough time to work up a case of nerves," Jessie said.

She kissed her mother good-bye and walked down the hall to ring for the elevator. There were two women in it, jabbering away a mile a minute. Jessie wasn't paying any attention to them because she was thinking that right after school she would have to do some marketing for Simba. Then she heard one of the women say something about a cat burglar. Last night the cat burglar had struck again. Apartment 12B, the Carlsons. It made Jessie's heart stand still. She was so frightened for Simba that she almost went back upstairs to see if Simba was still there.

She pulled herself together and told herself

that she was being silly. It was less than five minutes ago that she had said good-bye to Simba, and cat burglars did their dirty work at night. So Jessie relaxed some, but she thought about it all the way to school. How could anyone be so cruel as to steal cats? And how could anyone steal cats in the Tudor Towers? Were other people hiding cats there? Well, the Carlsons in 12B had obviously been doing just that. But how had the cat burglar known about it? It made Jessie shudder, but she went on her way.

Christmas Cove Elementary School was surrounded by palm trees and all kinds of flowering bushes. It looked more like a resort motel than a school. Jessie had to admit it was the best-looking school she had ever seen.

Her mother had enrolled her the week before. Her teacher was Mr. Reynolds in room 11. The halls were crowded with noisy kids. Her mother had told her how to find room 11. Turn right at the cafeteria, then it was the third door on the left. She found the cafeteria all right. Then she was confused. Maybe her mother had said it was the other way around. Turn left here, then it was the third door on the right. She should have made a note of it.

"Lost?"

Jessie turned to see a boy smiling at her. A boy almost half a foot taller than she was.

31

"Well, I know where I am," she said.

"Then you're not lost," said the boy, looking disappointed.

"But I don't know where I'm going, so I guess I am lost," she said. "I'm looking for Mr. Reynolds's class."

"What's your name?"

"Jessica Haskell," she said. "It's my first day."

"I thought so," the boy said. "You live in the Tudor Towers, don't you?"

"How did you guess?"

"I didn't," the boy said. "I live there too. I saw you arriving yesterday. I'm Carlos Rodriguez."

Jessie thought Carlos Rodriguez was very definitely among the cutest boys she had ever seen. In addition to being tall, he had short curly hair. He also dressed better than most of the other boys his age. Then Jessie remembered the name Rodriguez and she didn't feel so happy any more.

"Is your father the manager of the Tudor Towers?" she asked, hoping with all her heart that he was not.

"Yes, he is," Carlos said. "I'm glad we're neighbors."

"You and your father? That's nice. And convenient too."

Carlos laughed. So did Jessie.

"I meant you and me," Carlos said. "We're also

classmates. I'm in Mr. Reynolds's sixth grade too."

Carlos led the way down the hall to the right. It was still filled with other kids scurrying toward their rooms, but Jessie didn't notice them. She was feeling sorry that the man who enforced dumb rules about pets could have a son as cute as Carlos.

"Where are you from?" Carlos asked.

"Toronto," Jessie said. "Canada."

"Since you're the new girl in town, maybe I could give you the grand Christmas Cove tour."

"Hey, that would be great," Jessie said.

"In the afternoon," Carlos said. "Right after Trash for Cash."

"Trash for Cash?" Jessie asked. "What's that?"

"It's what I'm doing to raise money for the new gym equipment," Carlos said. "I collect old tin cans and take them over to the recycling plant on Poinciana Boulevard. You could go with me after school."

"This afternoon?"

"I do Trash for Cash every Monday and Tuesday after school," Carlos explained. "After the weekend is the best time for it."

"I don't think I can make it this afternoon."

"It's for a good cause," he said.

"It's just that I'm busy this afternoon," Jessie said. "I've got an errand to run."

34

"First I'll go with you," Carlos said.

Jessie wanted to tell him that he was more than welcome to go with her, but she couldn't. No one from the Tudor Towers could know that she was buying cat food that afternoon, especially the son of the condo manager.

"I'm sorry," she said. "I've got to run this errand all by myself."

She gave him her friendliest, sorriest smile. It didn't work. The smile on Carlos's face turned into a frown.

"Maybe tomorrow?" she asked.

"I don't know," he said. "I guess I'll see you around."

As they entered room 11, he walked away from her to some boys looking out the window. Jessie felt awful. It was the first time Simba had ever come between her and a boy.

Chapter 5

3:26 P.M., MONDAY

All through her first day at Christmas Cove Elementary School, Jessie thought that of all the bad luck in the world, she was having the worst. Even before the first bell had rung, she had scared off the cutest boy in the class. For the rest of the day when she should have been listening to Mr. Reynolds or trying to memorize the names of the other kids in the class, she had worried about cat burglars.

After school, as she walked by herself to the supermarket, she looked up and down and across the street to make sure that no one from the Tudor Towers was around. The coast was clear. Once inside the store, pushing a wire cart in front of her, she patrolled each and every aisle. The coast was still clear.

She wheeled the cart to the dog and cat food department. She reached out for seven cans of

Simba's favorite brand and her hands froze in midair. She had heard a familiar voice.

It was the voice of one of the ladies in the elevator this morning. She had greeted another shopper and was coming down the aisle toward Jessie. If the lady remembered her and saw her buying cat food, the jig would be up.

Quickly Jessie turned away from the cat food shelf. Desperately she began snatching things off shelves, anything at all. The basket was filled with groceries. The lady stopped beside her.

"Hello, there," she said to Jessie. "Don't I know you? Oh, yes, the elevator this morning."

"Yes, hello," Jessie said, dropping a jar of marshmallow whip into her cart.

"Welcome to Tudor Towers! I'm Mrs. Lomask, 9D. Doing the marketing for your mother?"

"Yes," Jessie said. "Yes, I am."

Mrs. Lomask glanced at Jessie's basket and looked puzzled. "Do you often do the marketing for your mother?"

"Not often," she said. "But tonight I'm cooking dinner. It's going to be a surprise."

Mrs. Lomask looked down into the basket again. "Marshmallow whip," she said. "Maraschino cherries, pistachios, chocolate fudge sauce, and sardines! I'm sure dinner will be quite a surprise." Mrs. Lomask laughed, patted Jessie on the head, and wheeled her cart away.

The minute she was gone, Jessie put all the things in her cart back on the shelves. Then, making sure no one was around, she went back and got the cat food, a flea collar, and a bag of Kitty Litter for the cardboard box she had improvised in the bathroom.

As soon as she was outside again, Jessie stuffed Simba's groceries into her book bag and walked back to Tudor Towers. She crossed the front lawn and walked by the pool. Simba had been all alone for seven hours. Jessie walked a little faster.

"Hello, young lady! Won't you join us?"

Jessie knew who it was without looking, but she looked anyway and she was right. It was Mr. Smith-Jones, spelled with a hyphen, in 17A. He was sunbathing with his wife, Mrs. Smith-Jones. They were English.

Her mother had introduced her to them in the lobby last night. She had liked them right away. Mr. Smith-Jones was so jolly fat and Mrs. Smith-Jones was so jolly skinny that they made her feel jolly too. She would have enjoyed joining them now, but she had more important things to do.

"I can't join you now," Jessie said. "Not today."

"Oh, do sit down for a bit, my dear," Mrs. Smith-Jones said.

Jessie was about to say no when she thought of something important the Smith-Joneses might

39

help her with. "Well, all right," she said. "For a bit."

"You're Jessie, right?" Mr. Smith-Jones said.

"Yes," Jessie said.

"And how old are you, Jessie?" Mrs. Smith-Jones asked.

"I'm going to be twelve soon," she said. "On Saturday."

"Oh, twelve on Saturday," Mr. Smith-Jones said, turning to his wife. "Make a note of that, Milly."

"I already have, Sydney," his wife said, and turned to Jessie. "And how are you going to celebrate your birthday?"

"We're going to have dinner in a restaurant and then go to a movie," Jessie said.

"How nice," Mrs. Smith-Jones said. "And what is your favorite color, Jessica?"

"Blue," Jessie said. She meant the shade of blue that matched Simba's eyes, but she couldn't mention that, of course. She had a feeling that she was going to get a blue birthday present from the Smith-Joneses. Feeling secretly pleased, Jessie decided to change the subject and ask them about her problem.

"Is it true," she asked, quoting Mrs. Lomask, "that the cat burglar struck again last night—the Carlsons, 12B?"

"Oh, yes," Mrs. Smith-Jones said. "Frightening, isn't it?"

"Awful," Jessie agreed. "But I don't understand. How can he steal cats when no pets are allowed here?"

Mr. and Mrs. Smith-Jones looked at each other in amazement, then burst into hearty laughter. Mrs. Smith-Jones was able to speak first.

"My dear child, the cat burglar doesn't steal cats. He steals money and precious jewels."

"And negotiable bonds," her husband said. "Oh, he's a rascal and a fiend."

"Oh," said Jessie, vastly relieved. "But why is he called the cat burglar?"

"Because he can scale our walls as well as a cat can scale a fence," Mr. Smith-Jones said.

"And he's quick and clever as a cat too," Mrs. Smith-Jones said.

"Thank you for explaining that to me," Jessie said. She got up to go, then sat down again. The Smith-Joneses had solved a big part of her cat problem. The least she could do was spend some time with them.

"Why do you have two names?" she asked. "Smith and Jones?"

Mr. Smith-Jones chuckled and patted his big stomach. "I suppose," he said, "because there is so much of me."

41

"That's not why," Jessie said, laughing at his joke.

"Many English people have double names," he explained. "And in my profession it was good to have a special name."

"What was your profession?" Jessie asked.

"The circus," Mr. Smith-Jones answered.

"The circus?" Jessie asked. She was about to ask if he had been the fat man but she caught herself in time. "What did you do in the circus?"

"I was the lion tamer," he said. "Of course, I've put on a few pounds since then."

"Quite a few," his wife said. "Oh, Jessie. You should have seen him then. So handsome! All of us girls in the circus were mad about him!"

"You were in the circus too?" Jessie asked. She almost asked if she had been the thin woman. "What were you?"

"I was the high trapeze artist," she said. "Of course, I've lost a few pounds since then."

"Quite a few," her husband said. "But you should have seen her, my dear. All the boys were mad for her."

"How exciting!" Jessie said. "And now you've retired to Florida. Do you like it here?"

"We love it," Mr. Smith-Jones said, smiling at his wife. "Don't we, Milly?"

"Yes, Sydney," she replied. "We absolutely adore it."

It was time now for Jessie to check in with Simba. She didn't tell Mr. and Mrs. Smith-Jones that, of course. Instead she just excused herself and said good-bye.

The apartment was quiet and empty. David was giving her mother a golf lesson.

First thing, Jessie hurried to her room and opened the bathroom door. "Simba!" she called, and there Simba was. It was lovely not worrying about her being stolen. It was enough to worry about David and her mother discovering her and banishing her forever from the Tudor Towers.

Simba woke up from her afternoon nap. She stood up on the bath mat and stretched. Then she came to Jessie. "Thank heavens you're safe," Jessie said as she picked Simba up and patted her neck. "Safe from the cat burglar and safe from Mom and David."

Knowing that the two golfers would not be around for a while longer, she gave Simba the run of the apartment. How else was Simba going to get all the exercise she needed? Jessie left the door to her room open and walked to the kitchen. She opened a can of the cat food and spooned it onto a saucer. It was while she was carrying the saucer to the living room that she heard the crash and saw Simba leaping to the traverse rod above the terrace draperies.

43

On the floor lay a dozen roses and the iron-stone pitcher that had been in her mother's family for generations. With a little luck it would remain there several generations more. Minus its handle, though, which lay broken in half a dozen pieces. Scolding Simba would do no good. Bright as she was, Simba didn't understand about heirlooms, especially when they got in the way of her most spectacular leaps.

Jessie rested the saucer on the floor and returned the intact part of the pitcher to the sideboard. She put the roses back into it and scraped up the pieces of the handle and took them back to the kitchen. As she threw the pieces in the garbage, she noticed the empty can of cat food on the counter. She threw that in the garbage too. It was the sort of near miss that made Jessie shudder for Simba's security. She had only thirteen more days left to permanently solve the problem.

Chapter 6

10:17 P.M., MONDAY

It was a dark night, pitch black dark. No moon. No stars.

It was an ideal night for the cat burglar.

But not wanting to take unnecessary chances, the cat burglar was dressed all in black. Black stretch pants, a tight black sweater, black gloves, and a black stocking cap as a face mask.

The cat burglar was striking again.

From high above, the black-clad figure leaped to the terrace of 15C, tiptoed across the terrace to the living room door—unlocked, as expected —crossed the living room to the hall door, and waited for the signal. In another moment, it came. Two quiet taps, a pause, then three more quiet taps. That was it, the signal. Right on schedule. Tonight, as almost always, the timing of the cat burglar was perfect. And so was the timing of the cat burglar's partner in crime.

The cat burglar unlocked the door and opened it.

A portly but not very jolly man, carrying a shopping bag, stepped through the doorway.

The cat burglar silently closed the door behind her husband.

"I see you found the terrace door still unlocked," he said.

"Yes," his wife said. "The Wendells really should be more careful. Doesn't say much for the military, I'm afraid."

Earlier in the evening they had called on Colonel Wendell and his wife. While they had pretended to admire the ocean view from the terrace door, Mr. Smith-Jones had unlocked it.

That was their usual technique. When they learned that a certain tenant would not be at home on a certain night, they would pay a social visit on the evening of that certain night and unlock the terrace door when no one was looking.

"And you, my little trapeze artist," Mr. Smith-Jones said, "I hope you ran into no trouble on the balconies."

"None, none at all," Mrs. Smith-Jones said.

"Well, then," Mr. Smith-Jones said as he rubbed his fat hands together greedily, "let us proceed."

In the bedroom Mr. Smith-Jones put on a pair

of gloves so that he wouldn't leave any finger prints. Then he flicked on a pencil flashlight. Together he and his wife searched the room. With their years of experience searching other people's rooms, they did their usual expert job.

Tonight they got a big haul, since Colonel and Mrs. Wendell were rich. In the bedroom the Smith-Joneses found a string of pearls, three diamond rings, a pair of gold cuff links, a platinum wrist watch, and three hundred and seventy-six dollars in cash. In the living room they found three priceless jade figurines and six silver loving cups. In the dining room they found a whole set of heirloom silver. They congratulated each other on a splendid night's work.

Now Mr. Smith-Jones took a long black velvet cloak from his shopping bag and handed it to his wife. While he packed the bag with all the stolen goods, she peeled off the black stocking cap, fluffed her hair, and put on the long velvet cloak over her cat burglar suit.

Then they strolled arm in arm down the corridor to the elevator. As they got off the elevator at their floor, an elderly man got on.

"Good evening, Mr. and Mrs. Smith-Jones," he said.

It was Mr. Kramer, 17F.

"Good evening, Mr. Kramer," Mr. Smith-

47

Jones said. "Are you taking a little stroll before retiring for the night?"

"A very short stroll," Mr. Kramer said. "It's a black night out. A fine night for a murder."

"Yes, isn't it," Mr. Smith-Jones said.

"Or a fine night for the cat burglar," Mr. Kramer said.

"Yes, isn't it," Mr. and Mrs. Smith-Jones said together.

After the elevator door closed behind Mr. Kramer, they smiled at each other. Yes, it had indeed been a fine night for the cat burglar. A few minutes later in their apartment, over cups of hot tea, they were still smiling.

"Well, my dear," Mr. Smith-Jones said, "who's next on our list?"

"14F, my dear."

"Oh, yes, the apartment of our little friend what's-her-name."

"Jessica. Saturday's her birthday, remember? Her folks are taking her out for dinner and the theater. We shall be able to work at our leisure."

"Tomorrow morning," Mr. Smith-Jones said, "you must get Jessica a lovely birthday present."

"Something lovely, yes," his wife said, "for a lovely little girl."

Mr. and Mrs. Smith-Jones chuckled. Then they laughed out loud at their own cleverness and had another cup of tea.

Chapter 7

4:12 P.M., TUESDAY

Carlos Rodriguez sat on the esplanade, looking out to sea through his binoculars. But he wasn't really paying much attention to the cruise ship, the tanker, or the freighter on the horizon. He was thinking about Jessica Haskell.

Almost one hundred years ago, Carlos's great-grandfather had sailed from Spain to Havana, Cuba. Then Carlos's grandfather had come from Cuba to Miami, Florida. His father was born in Miami, but his mother was born in Cuba. She met his father when she had visited relatives in Florida.

Most of Carlos's family—his cousins, aunts, and uncles and his grandmother Rodriguez—lived in Florida now, but they still spoke as much Spanish as English when they were together. So did Carlos. Sometimes he found himself thinking in Spanish. He was doing that now, because he was thinking about his grandmother, his *abuela,* and his two aunts, *las dos tías.*

As long as he could remember, they kept telling him what a *bonito* little boy he was, then what a *guapo* big boy he was. Lately, they had started to compare him to movie stars. His *tía* Maria thought he looked like Burt Reynolds. His *tía* Carmen thought he looked more like John Travolta. His *abuela* said he reminded her of Rudolph Valentino. Later Carlos had found out that in the 1920s Rudolph Valentino was considered the most handsome romantic man who ever lived.

Carlos had to laugh. He was thinking about Jessica Haskell again. Man, he had certainly not knocked her eyes out. He had introduced himself to her, helped her when she was lost, and offered to show her around Christmas Cove. He had even invited her to help him with Trash for Cash, something he had not done for any other girl. But that Haskell girl sure had shot him down. She hadn't even had the common decency to come up with a good excuse. A mysterious errand she couldn't talk about. What kind of excuse was that, anyway?

What had gone wrong?

Maybe it was his aunts and his grandmother who were wrong. Or maybe he was losing his looks. He wasn't aging well. But for sure that

Haskell girl didn't think he was a combination of Burt, John, and Rudolph. She thought he was a nothing. Forget her, he told himself. Don't give her another thought. It was just too bad she was so pretty.

Besides, he had better things to do than think of that Haskell girl. His Trash for Cash project, for instance. Carlos walked to the condominium and took the service elevator to the basement. When he reached the refuse room, he started going through all of yesterday's plastic trash bags, tossing the cans into a pile in the corner. Maybe he had gone wrong by inviting Jessie to join him in trashing and cashing. That mightn't have sounded like a very neat thing to do, rooting through rubbish down in a cellar. Especially to a beautiful girl like her. Hey, he angrily told himself. Forget about her. Don't give her another thought. She doesn't exist.

He opened the last plastic bag. He pulled out a Coke can and a can of tuna fish and threw them in the pile. He worked his way through the rest of the bag. Then one particular can caught his eye. In all his afternoons of going through the garbage, he had never seen another one like it. The can was a cat food can, and that could mean only one thing. Someone at the Tudor Towers was keeping a cat!

Carlos wasn't about to throw this particular

can in the recycling pile. This can was evidence. He put the bag it had come from in another corner and ran upstairs to his father's office, which was just off the main lobby.

Almost a thousand people lived in the Tudor Towers. Managing it was a lot like running a small city. In addition to the janitors and the gardeners and the doormen and the pool keeper, three secretaries worked there. Carlos said hello to all three of them as he marched into his father's office.

Mr. Rodriguez was resting the phone in the receiver. "What is it?" he asked. From the expression on his father's face, Carlos could tell that he was in a very serious mood.

"A cat food can!" Carlos said excitedly. "Believe it or not, Dad, an empty cat food can. I found it in the trash!"

"You've got to be wrong," Mr. Rodriguez said.

"Read the label," Carlos said. "Someone here is keeping a cat."

Mr. Rodriguez looked at the can and nodded in dismay. As though his regular workload wasn't already enough, the cat burglar had struck again. Last night Colonel and Mrs. Wendell had been robbed. All day long he had received one complaint after another from nervous tenants. And now on top of the cat burglar, there was a cat. If it wasn't so serious, the coincidence would have been funny.

"What are we going to do, Dad?"

"I don't know what we *can* do," Mr. Rodriguez said. "We can't go around accusing the tenants, searching their apartments. Besides, I'm getting it from all sides about the cat burglar. I don't have time to find a cat, Carlos."

Carlos wished there was some way he could help, but it wasn't until he was watching TV that night that the inspiration hit him.

He had seen enough detectives at work on television to know how to be one himself. Tomorrow morning he would start working on his first case. But he wouldn't tell his father. He would surprise him.

Being a detective was going to be his new career. It was glamorous and exciting. It would do wonders for his image: girls were always falling all over themselves for private eyes. Even girls like . . . no forget her, he told himself.

No, not quite, he thought. Wait a minute.

Maybe when he had caught whoever was keeping a cat in the Tudor Towers and brought them to justice, Jessie Haskell would be so impressed that she would give him a second chance. Somehow he just couldn't forget about her.

Chapter 8

8:50 A.M., SATURDAY

While Simba sat in her closet gulping down her morning cat food, Jessie and her mother and David were eating their breakfast on the terrace overlooking the Atlantic Ocean. Because it was Saturday, they were dressed casually. Jessie was wearing a swim suit, her mother was wearing a blouse and jeans, and David was wearing a polo shirt and a pair of plaid shorts.

"What would you like to do today?" David asked as he put the paper down on the table and took a sip of his coffee.

"Nothing much," Jessie said. "Maybe I'll work on my tan some."

"On your birthday?" David asked. "I was thinking of something more special than that."

"But you've already made plans for tonight," Jessie said. "Dinner and the movies. That's special."

"Why don't we go see jai alai," her mother suggested. "Or an exhibition baseball game."

"The aquarium's terrific," David said.

"I don't think so," Jessie said.

"But Jessie . . ." her mother said.

"You two go somewhere," Jessie said. "You're the newlyweds. I thought newlyweds liked being alone together."

"It would be more fun if you joined us," David said.

"Thanks, but no thanks," Jessie said. "You go out and have fun. I'll stay here."

Jessie stood up and started to clear the table. David and her mother were trying so hard to make them a family that it made her sad not to join in. But Simba hadn't had the run of the apartment for almost three days. If she didn't get some exercise, she was going to get restless.

"You're not trying to get rid of us, are you?" David asked.

"That's it exactly," Jessie said. "There are some details for the wedding present surprise I've got to work on. And I'll need the living room for it."

"Not on your birthday," her mother said. "It's your day."

"I only need an hour or two, Mom," Jessie said. "So come on, you guys. Scram. Vamoose. Get lost. I love you."

David and her mother smiled. Jessie was glad that she hadn't hurt their feelings.

While she was stacking the dishwasher, she heard the front door slam. They were gone. Jessie opened the door to her room and called for Simba. A moment later Simba ran into the living room.

While Simba was investigating the chairs and the sofa and considering her first major leap of the day, the doorbell rang. Simba leaped from the sofa to the living room floor as quickly as a fireman on his way to a three-alarmer.

"Good, Simba," Jessie whispered.

Simba raced ahead of her into the bedroom. She hid herself in the bathroom. Jessie closed the door. Then she ran back to the living room. She made sure that Simba had left no telltale signs. It was okay. None of her toys was on the floor.

The doorbell rang again. Jessie answered it.

"Who are you?" a little boy asked.

"I'm Jessica Haskell. Who are you?"

"I'm Herman Riley. 4G."

Herman Riley, 4G, was about nine years old and almost four feet tall. He probably weighed more than thirty pounds, but he didn't look it. He wore sunglasses so large that all the face Jessie could see was the tip of a nose, a mouth, and under it some chin, but not much.

57

"Is the lady of the house at home?" Herman asked.

"My mother's out now," Jessie replied. "Will I do?"

Herman shook his head. "Nothing personal, you understand," he said.

"Do you want to come in and wait for her?" Jessie asked.

"Okay," Herman said. "I'll wait."

Jessie wished at once that she hadn't let Herman in. Simba needed all the running time she could get to herself. "Would you like to sit down?"

"No, thank you," Herman said. "This isn't a social call."

"Then I guess you won't want a Coke or anything."

"I'm on a diet," Herman said.

"A diet?" Jessie asked. "You're on a diet?"

"Not a weight-reducing diet," Herman said. "A dental diet. To reduce cavities. I'm anti-sugar."

"How much do you weigh, Herman?"

"Forty-three pounds," Herman said, and sneezed.

Jessie thought that if she weighed forty-three pounds, she would probably be antiviolence too. "May I ask what brings you here?"

"I'm selling Girl Scout cookies," Herman said,

and sneezed again. "I don't eat them, of course. I just sell them."

"I thought only Girl Scouts sold Girl Scout cookies," Jessie said.

"I'm selling them for my sister," Herman said. "She's the Girl Scout in the family."

"What a thoughtful brother you must be," Jessie said.

"I'm working on commission. She gives me a dime for every box I sell. Would you like to place an order?"

"Gee, I don't know," Jessie said.

"Okay, I'll wait for Mrs. Haskell," Herman said.

"My last name's Haskell," Jessie said. "My mother's name is Mrs. Bradley."

"I'll wait for Mrs. Bradley then," Herman said. Then he sneezed. Three times.

"That's a terrible cold you have, Herman," Jessie said.

"I don't have a cold," he said. "I'm allergic."

"Allergic to what?"

"Cats."

"Cats!" Jessie said. "Oh, no!"

"That's the reason we live in this building," Herman said. "They don't allow cats here." Herman sneezed five more times. He looked at Jessie suspiciously. "You don't have a cat here, do you?"

"Why, Herman," Jessie said. "You know cats aren't allowed here. You said so yourself."

"But I never sneeze unless there's a cat around."

"Maybe you're allergic to something else besides cats."

"Like what?"

Jessie looked desperately around the room. Her eyes fell on the ironstone pitcher. Even minus its handle, her mother still treasured it and kept red roses in it. Simba treasured it, too, and when she had the run of the house, she liked to nestle up against the soft flowers.

"Well," Jessie said, "like roses, maybe."

"I don't think so," Herman said. "I never sneezed in a garden unless a cat's been there."

"Let's see anyway," Jessie said. She went and got the pitcher and brought it over to Herman. He sneezed at it. Again and again.

"Are you sure about no cats here?" he asked.

"Unless you're allergic to flowers, you must be coming down with something, Herman," she said anxiously. "Why don't you go home and go to bed, Herman."

"I've got to wait for Mrs. Bradley," he said.

"Why don't you put me down for half a dozen boxes of the cookies," Jessie said. "I'm sure it'll be okay with my mother."

"Just half a dozen?"

61

"Make it a dozen," Jessie said. "Any flavor. It doesn't matter. Just go home. Now. I'm sure you'll feel better in no time."

"Thanks," Herman said. "You'll get the cookies in a couple of weeks. My sister does the deliveries."

As Jessie held the front door open for him, Herman sneezed again.

"Gee," he said. "Maybe we'll have to move someplace where they don't allow flowers either."

Then he sneezed a good-bye and walked down the hall toward the elevator.

Jessie heaved a big sigh. She was awfully glad that Herman hadn't looked more closely at the roses. Her mother had brought them back from Mexico and they were made of paper.

Chapter 9

9:32 A.M., SATURDAY

While Jessie was sighing her sigh of relief, Carlos Rodriguez was spending his Saturday morning sleeping. Not just sleeping, though. He was dreaming a dream so wonderful that it curved a big, happy grin all over his face.

He was dreaming that he had been named Detective of the Year. The White House lawn was jammed with hundreds of people from all over the United States and Canada. The camera crews of all three national networks were there. Broadcasting live, of course. And by satellite to Europe and South America. The President of the United States was in the middle of his presentation speech.

He was praising Carlos so highly that it made Carlos blush in his sleep. First he told about Carlos solving the Incredible Cat Caper. Then he went on to tell about Carlos's next two cases, the

First National Bank Robbery and the Rich Heiress Kidnapping. Now he was just finishing the fantastic story of how Carlos had solved the Stolen Government Plans Mystery. Then he pinned a medal on Carlos.

The crowd cheered.

Then a girl about Carlos's age ducked under a Secret Service man's arm and ran up to him. She threw her arms around him.

The girl was Jessie Haskell.

Jessie kissed him.

And the crowd cheered.

It was the roaring of the crowd that woke Carlos from his dream. He closed his eyes again and enjoyed thinking about the dream. After he solved the Incredible Cat Caper, there was no reason why he couldn't go on being a private eye and solving all kinds of sensational and baffling cases.

And he *might* win a medal.

Carlos jumped out of bed and got dressed. If he was going to make his dream come true, he wasn't going to be able to spend his Saturday mornings in bed anymore.

He ran to the basement and retrieved the garbage bag he had left in the corner earlier in the week. He pulled out all its contents and made a list of them.

1. Empty cat food can

2. Empty coffee tin

3. Magazine section of *The Miami Herald* with crossword half done

4. Flattened tube of toothpaste

5. Six little pieces of broken china

6. A pair of worn-out golf shoes, male, size 10

7. Empty soap powder box

8. Three empty Coke cans

9. Paper towels, napkins, match boxes, etc.

Carlos thought some. Then feeling very professional, he made a new list of possible clues.

1. *Miami Herald*

2. Golf shoes

3. Broken china

Carlos's next move was to talk with Jack, the day doorman. Jack told him that half of the tenants at the Tudor Towers had *The Miami Herald* delivered to their doors. Carlos guessed that his first clue wasn't a very helpful one. He would have to do better with clue number two. What men at the Tudor Towers played golf?

After two hours of investigation, Carlos wondered if he would be a very old man before he had cracked his first case. He was even wondering if he should just give up. As he passed by his father's office, he heard Colonel Wendell raising the roof about the cat burglar.

"I have figured out our loss, sir," the colonel

was shouting. "It is well over ten thousand dollars."

"I'm very sorry, Colonel," Mr. Rodriguez said.

"Not to mention the items of sentimental value, like my trophies, which are priceless."

"I understand your feelings, Colonel."

"My wife is a nervous wreck, sir. She's terrified. All the tenants are terrified. Who knows when or where the cat burglar will strike again?"

"No one knows when, Colonel. It's a rough situation."

"May I ask, sir, why no progress has been made to apprehend the burglar and recover my stolen property?"

"These things take time," Mr. Rodriguez said. "The police are doing their best."

"The police!" cried the Colonel. "What steps have *you* taken to protect the tenants' property and their very lives?"

"As of tonight, we're doubling the guard."

"And how many guards does that make, sir?"

"Four," Mr. Rodriguez said. "Two policemen from Christmas Cove and two private guards that I've hired. There will be a man stationed at every corner of the building. The cat burglar won't get past them, Colonel."

"He had better not, sir! If this thieving doesn't stop, heads are going to start rolling around here. And the first may well be yours, sir!"

Carlos couldn't bear to listen to his father having to be polite to a bully like Colonel Wendell. It was humiliating. Even so, Carlos knew that his father wouldn't let Colonel Wendell intimidate him. His father wasn't a quitter.

Carlos knew he wasn't going to be a quitter either. He gathered up the fragments of broken china and studied them. Then he got out his model cement and glued them together. He thought it must have been the handle to a pitcher or a bowl. He decided it looked more like a pitcher handle. It could be that the owner had thrown away the broken handle and still had the rest of the pitcher in his apartment.

How could he go about investigating that?

It was a tough one.

Carlos took a long walk on the beach to think that one over. But afterwards he still didn't know what he was supposed to do next.

He wasn't discouraged, though. He bet Magnum P.I. didn't solve his first case overnight either.

Chapter 10

6:14 P.M., SATURDAY

That evening, Jessie was ready to go to dinner and the movies. Even though she was looking forward to both, she wasn't very happy. Only seven days left and she still hadn't figured a solution to her and Simba's problem. Every time she thought of something that might be okay, she thought of two reasons why it wasn't.

"Jessie," her mother called from the bedroom, "will you lock the terrace door?"

"I already have," Jessie called back.

Then the doorbell rang.

Since the appearance of Herman Riley that morning, Jessie had decided that opening the front door was not in her—or Simba's—best interests. But she had no choice. She went to the door and took a deep breath. She lifted a hand that was as heavy as lead and opened the door.

It wasn't Herman Riley.

It was the Smith-Joneses.

And what Mrs. Smith-Jones was bearing was obviously a gift.

"Happy birthday, Jessica," Mrs. Smith-Jones said.

"Happy birthday, my dear little twelve-year-old," her husband said.

"Thank you!" Jessica said. "Please come in."

"But only for a moment," Mr. Smith-Jones said. "We know you have a very important engagement tonight."

"Jess," her mother called from the bedoom, "who is it?"

"Mr. and Mrs. Smith-Jones," Jessie called back.

"Oh," her mother said, "will you explain?"

Before Jessie said a word, Mr. Smith-Jones called toward the bedroom, "No explanation necessary, Mrs. Bradley. You are dressing for a very important engagement. Dinner and the theater. We are only staying for a moment at the very most."

"But please," Jessie's mother called back, "come again and stay longer."

"We certainly will," Mr. Smith-Jones called. "Thank you, Mrs. Bradley." He and his wife knowingly eyed one another. They were going to accept Mrs. Bradley's invitation a lot sooner than she could expect.

"What a lovely room," Mrs. Smith-Jones said as

she inspected it. "So beautifully furnished and decorated. Who is your mother's decorator, Jessica?"

"My mother," Jessie replied. "She did it all herself."

"What a gorgeous view," Mrs. Smith-Jones said as she turned toward the terrace.

"Yes, isn't it?" Mr. Smith-Jones said. He followed his wife to the terrace door and looked over her shoulder.

"Look at all those delightful sailboats!" Mrs. Smith-Jones said.

"Would you like to go out on the terrace?" Jessie asked.

"Oh, no, dear, we must be off," Mr. Smith-Jones said.

"The gift," he said. "You haven't given Jessica her birthday present."

"Happy birthday, Jessica," Mrs. Smith-Jones said as she handed her the package.

"Oh, you shouldn't have," Jessie said, although she was glad that they had.

"Just a little something," Mrs. Smith-Jones said. "Don't open it until you're ready for bed."

"Oh, I won't," Jessie said, already planning to take a peek. "Thank you very much."

"Bless you, my dear," Mr. Smith-Jones said. "Come along, Milly."

"Many happy returns," Mrs. Smith-Jones said.

She gave Jessie a kiss on each cheek. "Come along, Sydney."

As soon as the Smith-Joneses were gone, Jessie opened the present. It was a beautiful pale blue nightgown. Her mother would have said it was much too sophisticated for a twelve-year-old which made it just perfect for Jessie. It made her feel as though she really was a year older.

An hour later, while Jessie and her mother and David were safely dipping into their shrimp cocktail five miles away, Mrs. Smith-Jones, in her thief's uniform, swung safely onto the balcony of 14F. She found the terrace door as she had left it, unlocked. In a moment she was at the corridor door, waiting for the signal from her accomplice. The three sharp taps came almost immediately. In another instant Mrs. Smith-Jones opened the door and let Mr. Smith-Jones into the apartment. In another instant they were both hard at work in the master bedroom.

They searched the room thoroughly, doing their usual expert job. They carefully examined every square inch of the closets and every square inch of the drawers and the bed tables and the lady's dressing table.

When they were finished, Mr. Smith-Jones held up a string of pearls. That was it. For all their effort, just a string of pearls. Mr. Smith-Jones was indignant.

"Ridiculous," he snorted, his chubby face flushed an angry red. "Our breaking in here has been a sheer waste of time!"

"How dare they!" his wife demanded. She was even more furious than her husband. "How dare they live in an expensive apartment like this and not have some valuable jewelry and a sizable amount of ready cash within easy reach! It just goes to show that you can't judge people by appearances."

"Hypocrites," Mr. Smith-Jones agreed. "I don't know what people are coming to. Well, should we search the other bedroom?"

"If there's nothing in the master bedroom," Mrs. Smith-Jones said, "there isn't likely to be anything in the girl's bedroom."

"I agree," Mr. Smith-Jones said, "but let us be thorough. At least we have our standards to live up to."

"Which is more than I can say for certain other people," Mrs. Smith-Jones said. "Yes, let us be thorough."

Her husband led the way across the living room, opened the door to the second bedroom, and stepped into it. He flashed his light around it. His light lit on the bed and held there.

Mr. Smith-Jones gasped.

73

"Why, it's a cat," he gasped.

"Impossible," his wife said in amazement. "It can't be a cat! Not in this building!"

"But it is a cat. A beautiful pussy cat," Mr. Smith-Jones said.

"Then it must be a doll cat," Mrs. Smith-Jones said. "In this building it has to be a doll cat. Not a real one."

At that moment, Simba decided to show that she was indeed a real cat. First she blinked and shook herself out of the sound sleep she had been enjoying. Then she stood up and bared her teeth and arched her back. She generally and completely showed her disapproval of these strange and unwelcome people. Whoever they were, Simba definitely did not like them or trust them.

"Well, well," Mr. Smith-Jones sighed. "No wonder that little brat Jessica was so curious about cat burglars. She's been harboring this delicious creature in her room all along."

"Quite against the rules too," Mrs. Smith-Jones said. "Children today, they have no respect for the law. Sometimes I wonder what the world is coming to, Sydney."

"But it's a beautiful cat," Mr. Smith-Jones said. "I love it."

"I don't think the cat is returning the compli-

74

ment, Sydney," his wife said. "The cat clearly finds you repulsive."

"Oh, I think it'll have a change of heart," Mr. Smith-Jones said. "These things take time."

"What, my dear?" Mrs. Smith-Jones asked. "What did you just say?"

"I want that cat, Milly," he cried. "I must have it for my very own."

"Impossible," Mrs. Smith-Jones said. "Where would we keep it?"

"Why, on my lap."

"Come to your senses," Mrs. Smith-Jones said. "It's against the rules and regulations of this building to keep cats. What kind of people do you think we are?"

"But that little brat Jessica keeps a cat," Mr. Smith-Jones said. "Why can't I?"

"What can you expect of people like that? People who do not have any valuable or decent jewelry will stoop to anything. Even to breaking the law by keeping a cat. Why do you need that cat, Sydney?"

"Milly," Mr. Smith-Jones said, his voice suddenly very sad. "It's not fair. It's been so long since I had a cat. Not since the circus. I miss them terribly. You keep up with your acrobatics, but what about me?"

"Please, Sydney," Mrs. Smith-Jones said. "Be reasonable."

76

"We won't be at the Tudor Towers much longer," he said. "If you do not let me have that beautiful cat, I will be miserable, Milly," he said. "Forever. And I shall never be happy again. Not ever."

"Very well." His wife sighed. "But why steal that one? I'll buy you one at a pet store."

"Oh, no," her husband said. "Cats like this one cost a bundle. I don't want just any cat."

"I think you've made a very convincing case for the cat," Mrs. Smith-Jones said. "You may keep the cat, Sydney."

"Oh, thank you, Milly," her husband said lovingly. Then he took a step toward Simba. "Come to me, my beautiful kitty cat. Come to Daddy."

Simba backed up against the wall.

"Yes, dear, you may keep the cat," Mrs. Smith-Jones said. "But not just yet. Not tonight."

"Whyever not? I must have that kitty cat immediately."

"No, my dear. Tomorrow night we have a date with the Lomasks. They're the richest people in the building. It promises to be our biggest haul. That's why we have saved it for last."

"So?"

"People are so odd about cats," Mrs. Smith-Jones said. "You never know what extremes people will go to to recover lost pets."

"But pets are illegal in the Tudor Towers," Mr.

77

Smith-Jones said. "They couldn't possibly complain to the authorities about the theft, could they?"

"No, they're not that dumb," his wife conceded. "But they might take the law into their own hands, Sydney. They might start a search. If they came to our apartment, how could we stop them without raising suspicion?"

"I see your point, Milly," her husband said. "But what are we going to do?"

"We'll simply have to make a return visit to the Bradleys," Mrs. Smith-Jones said. "The night after we pay a call on the Lomasks."

"That's a promise?" Mr. Smith-Jones asked.

"It's a promise," Mrs. Smith-Jones said. "In forty-eight hours you will have your cat and we will be gone forever."

"And South America, here we come," Mr. Smith-Jones said.

"It will be perfect," Mrs. Smith-Jones said. "I heard Mrs. Bradley talking to someone on the beach this morning. She said she and her husband were going to a dinner party the night after tomorrow. So we can easily get in here and steal your feline."

"I think we'd better leave, Milly," her husband said. "What if the Bradleys come back from dinner early?"

"Not so quickly," his wife said. She held up the

string of pearls they had stolen from Jessie's mother. "We have to return these to where we found them."

"Whatever for?" Mr. Smith-Jones asked.

"We don't want to put the Bradleys on their guard. It's no great loss, my dear. They're cultured."

In less than a minute the pearls were returned, drawers were closed. And the Smith-Joneses were happily on their way home.

Chapter 11

11:26 A.M., SUNDAY

The next morning Carlos decided on his next move toward nailing the guilty party who was keeping a cat in his apartment building. Last spring he had sold magazine subscriptions and earned enough money to buy himself a bike. Now he needed a cover for his next move. Posing as a magazine salesman would do the trick. Fortunately he still had his advertising pamphlets and order pads.

He rang the doorbell of apartment 4G.

Herman Riley opened the door.

"Hi, Herman," Carlos said. "Your mother or your father at home?"

"Hi, Carlos," Herman said. "No, they're not. They're out playing golf."

It was Carlos's first break in a long time. Investigating the Rileys' apartment without Mr. and Mrs. Riley there would be a snap.

"Herman," he said. "Can I come in and wait for your parents?"

"Sure, come on in," Herman said. "You want to buy some Girl Scout cookies while you're waiting?"

"Sorry," Carlos said. "I'm here to sell, not to buy."

While he pretended to admire the living room, Carlos looked all around for a pitcher that would match the handle he had in his pocket. There wasn't any kind of pitcher in the living room. He would have to think up an excuse to look in the other rooms.

"Hey, Herman, I'm sort of thirsty," Carlos said. "Could I have a glass of water?"

"Sure, sit down. I'll get it for you."

"No," Carlos said. "I'll come with you."

Going through the dining room, he didn't see the pitcher that he was looking for. In the kitchen, while Herman was getting him a glass of water, he drew the same blank. Now only the bedrooms were left for him to investigate.

Then Carlos had a disturbing thought. It would be easy enough to get Herman to show him through the rest of the Rileys' apartment, but what about the other suspects on the list? They weren't going to give a twelve-year-old kid a chance to investigate all their rooms. You, Carlos told himself, are in trouble again. Some detective he was turning out to be.

"Here's your water," Herman said.

"Thanks," Carlos said.

"What do you want to sell my mother and father?" Herman asked.

"Magazines," Carlos said. He held up his advertising material.

"Let me see your list," Herman said. "I like to read magazines. When I'm watching TV shows I don't like."

Carlos handed over the list and Herman read it.

"Here's one magazine I sure don't want," Herman said.

"Which one?" Carlos asked absentmindedly.

"All About Cats," Herman said. "I sure wouldn't want that one. I'm allergic to cats."

"You're *what?*"

"Allergic to cats," Herman repeated.

"You mean you can't be anywhere near them?" Carlos asked.

"That's right," Herman said.

"What happens to you?"

"I sneeze like there's no tomorrow," Herman said. "My doctor says someday it might just go away, but whenever I'm near a cat, I nearly sneeze my head off."

83

"You start sneezing as soon as you see a cat?" Carlos asked.

"I don't even have to see them," Herman said, not meaning to brag. "I can tell where they've been and where they're going."

Well, Carlos thought, at least that takes care of this apartment. The Rileys wouldn't have a cat. Mentally, he scratched 4G from his list.

Then Carlos had an inspiration.

"Herman," he said, "does your allergy ever fail you? I mean it *always* works?"

"Oh, always," Herman said. "I can guarantee you that."

"Great!" Carlos said. "Herman, I've got a business proposition for you. Have you ever thought of getting out of Girl Scout cookies and getting into magazines?"

"Girl Scout cookies have been very good to me," Herman said.

"But the future's in magazines, Herman," Carlos said. "We could be partners."

"I don't know," Herman said. "My sister gives me a dime for every box I sell."

"I'll double that," Carlos said. "Heck, I'll give you a quarter for every subscription we sell."

"Maybe I'm getting a little old to sell Girl Scout cookies," Herman said thoughtfully. "When do you want to start?"

84

"Now," Carlos said. "There isn't a moment to lose."

"Sure, partner," Herman said. "Who's next on the list?"

"Good morning, Mrs. Myers," Carlos said. "I'm Carlos Rodriguez."

"Oh, yes, the manager's son. Good morning, Carlos."

Mrs. Myers was a plump, friendly, happy-looking woman. She looked like a woman, Carlos thought, who might like cats.

"This is Herman Riley."

"Hello, Herman."

"Hello," Herman said.

"Mrs. Myers," Carlos said, "may we speak to you and Mr. Myers for a minute or two?"

"Mr. Myers is playing golf, but you can certainly speak to me. Come in."

Carlos made a note that Mr. Myers was a golfer.

They went into the living room and sat down.

"Would you boys like a Coke?" Mrs. Myers asked.

"No thank you," Herman said. "I'm against . . ."

"Yes, please," Carlos said quickly. Having a Coke would give Herman's allergy plenty of

85

time to act up if there was a cat hidden in the apartment.

"I'll just be a second," Mrs. Myers said, and went into the kitchen.

All the while she was gone, Carlos watched Herman carefully, but Herman didn't sneeze once. He didn't even look like he was beginning to feel terrible.

"Now, boys," Mrs. Myers said as she gave Carlos his Coke, "tell me what's on your minds."

"Herman and I are partners," Carlos said. "We're selling magazine subscriptions."

"Well! Isn't that enterprising of you! What magazines?"

Carlos gave her his list and she looked it over.

"Our Wide Wonderful World," Mrs. Myers read from the list. "I've heard of that magazine. It's all about nature, isn't it?"

"Yes, and it's a good one," Carlos said. "Very popular."

"Oh, I love nature," Mrs. Myers said. "But I don't know. My husband says I don't read half the magazines I subscribe to already."

Carlos stole another look at Herman. Still no sneezing. He looked fine. In fact, he looked better than when he first came in. Carlos decided there was no cat in this apartment.

He stood up. "Why don't you talk it over with

your husband, Mrs. Myers? There's no hurry. Let's go, Herman."

Carlos was just opening the door to the hall when he heard a really terrific sneeze behind him. He wheeled around; he had found the guilty party after all.

But Herman was just standing there not sneezing.

Mrs. Myers was blowing her nose.

"Excuse me," she said. "I'm afraid I'm catching a terrible cold."

Mr. and Mrs. Anderson got into an argument about which magazines to subscribe to and it took them ten minutes to come to a decision. That was plenty of time for Herman's allergy to go to work. It didn't; Herman didn't so much as sniffle, let alone sneeze. Carlos knew there was no cat in apartment 11F.

As the two boys walked down the corridor, Carlos was thinking that at last the case was narrowing down to fewer and fewer suspects. If he had only known about Herman the Hound earlier, this case would have been wrapped up long ago.

Then Herman interrupted Carlos's triumphant thoughts.

"Hey, what time is it?"

Carlos looked at his watch.

87

"Five after twelve. Why?"

"Holy cow," Herman yelped. "I'm late."

"Late for what?"

"My father's taking me to Miami! The Dolphin game. We're supposed to leave at twelve sharp. If I'm late, he's going to take my sister!"

"But you can't leave," Carlos said. "It's important."

"I'm sorry, Carlos, but we can sell magazine subscriptions anytime. Right?"

"This has nothing to do with magazine subscriptions," Carlos said before he could catch himself. "We're hunting down a criminal. Someone who's keeping a cat here against the rules and regulations of the Tudor Towers. We've narrowed the suspects down just a little. You can't leave when I'm on my way to cracking my first case."

"A cat in the Tudor Towers?" Herman asked. "You mean the magazines were just a cover?"

"Yeah," Carlos said. "You still want to be my partner?"

"You bet," Herman said.

"You'll have to skip the Dolphin game. I can't do it without your allergies."

"Who's next?" Herman asked.

"We'll start with the Morrisons," Carlos said. "Okay?"

Herman thought a minute. He should never

have let that girl tell him he was allergic to roses or that he was coming down with a cold.

"Skip the Morrisons," Herman shouted as he ran down the corridor to the elevator. "We're going to the Bradleys' to solve the case!"

Carlos followed close on Herman's heels. He couldn't wait to see the expression of Jessica Haskell's face when she heard that he had solved the Incredible Cat Caper at the Bradleys'. It had been less than a week since he had first met Jessie and he didn't know yet that she was Mr. Bradley's stepdaughter. Little did he know that Jessie wouldn't be at all happy to realize that Carlos was a supersleuth.

Chapter 12

11:36 A.M., SUNDAY

As Jessie opened the door, she blinked twice. She was surprised to see Herman Riley back so soon, but she was even more surprised to see that he was accompanied by Carlos Rodriguez. But surprised as she was, she wasn't half as surprised to see Carlos as Carlos was to see her.

"What are you doing here?" she asked.

"Selling magazine subscriptions," Carlos said numbly. "We're here to see the Bradleys. What are you doing here?"

"She lives here," Herman said. "I sold her a dozen boxes of Girl Scout cookies yesterday. She should be good for half a dozen magazine subscriptions too."

"But we're looking for the Bradleys' apartment," Carlos said. "This must be the Haskells'."

"Mrs. Bradley is my mother," Jessie said. "My stepfather is Mr. Bradley."

"I'm sorry," Carlos sighed. "I didn't know."

"That's not what he meant," Herman said. "He means he's sorry you live here. Nothing personal, of course. It's our first arrest."

"I thought you were selling magazine subscriptions," Jessie said.

"That was just a cover," Herman said. "May we come in?"

"If you're coming in to arrest me," Jessie said, "I'd rather you stayed outside."

"But we have to come in," Herman said. "For the evidence."

Carlos wished that Herman would shut up. For Jessie, it was all too ridiculous for her to even try to figure out.

"You wouldn't arrest one of your best customers, would you, Herman?" she asked.

"Don't try to play on my sympathies," Herman said. "We're here for justice."

"Not so fast, Herman," Carlos said. "Maybe we've made a mistake."

Then he saw the pitcher over on the sideboard. As he walked toward it, he pulled his valuable clue from his pocket. He put the broken pieces he had glued together against the side of the pitcher. Everything fit perfectly.

"Got all the proof you need?" Herman asked. "Did you bring some handcuffs?"

"Where did you get that handle?" Jessie asked.

All of a sudden, she had a sinking feeling that what Carlos was doing might not be so ridiculous. She had a feeling that the moment she had dreaded had finally arrived.

"I got them from the trash," Carlos said.

"Oh, no," Jessie sighed. "Trash for Cash?"

"Sorry," Carlos said.

"How dare you come here and talk about arresting me?" Jessie asked in dismay. "You can't lock someone up for breaking the handle on a pitcher."

"Confess, Miss Haskell," Herman said. "It'll be easier on you in the long run." Herman drew up his shoulders, closed his eyes, and let out the biggest sneeze that either Carlos or Jessie had ever heard. "That's it!" he screamed. "Don't tell me it's the roses. Where are you keeping it?"

"Keeping what, Herman?" Jessie asked, although she was afraid she knew the answer. "When is someone going to tell me what's going on?"

"A cat." Carlos said sadly. "You've been hiding one here, haven't you?"

Jessie felt her body go rigid with fright. Even if she had felt like admitting the truth, she couldn't have. The muscles in her throat were too tight for her to make sounds.

"The broken handle," Carlos said. "And

93

Herman's sneezing. I guess we don't need any more proof."

"What any of that has to do with a cat, I'll never know," Jessie said, trying hard to regain her breath. It was the least she could do for Simba.

"The cat food can," Carlos said. "It was in the same garbage bag with all the other things. That's how we know there's a cat in this apartment. Unless you have some explanation. I'm just starting out in the private eye business so I'm not perfect yet."

From the look on his face, Jessie knew that he was almost hoping he was making a mistake. For his sake, and for hers and Simba's, she just had to come up with some explanation.

"Well, I guess my secret is out in the open now," she said. "I should have known someone would find out sooner or later. The fact is that I happen to be hooked on cat food. I can't get enough of the stuff. It's so embarrassing. I hope you won't tell a soul, my mom and stepfather especially. If they ever found out, they'd probably send me to a psychiatrist."

At that very moment Simba stepped lightly into the living room. Of all the times for Jessie not to have made absolutely sure that the door to her room was shut, this was the worst. Simba walked toward Jessie and leaped into her arms.

94

"I knew it," Herman said as he began to sneeze.

"Simba," Jessie said sadly. "I want you to meet Carlos and Herman."

The two boys stared at Simba. As far as she was concerned, it was only her due. It had been far too long since she had had a chance to show off.

"These boys want to take you away from me," Jessie said. "Just because there's a stupid law in the Tudor Towers about no pets. Don't worry, Simba. They're not going to get away with it."

"I'm sorry, Jessie," Carlos said. "I was sorry the minute we walked in. I didn't make up the rule. I wish I'd never found that can of cat food. I was only trying to help my father."

Herman was once again building up to one of his sneezes. Just as he was about to let it get the best of him, Jessie's mother and David walked in.

As soon as Simba saw them, she leaped into Mrs. Bradley's arms.

"Oh, no," Mrs. Bradley said as she stroked Simba's head. "How on earth did you get here?"

"Let me introduce you to Carlos Rodriguez and Herman Riley," Jessie said. "They've come to arrest me."

"You boys can't take the law into your own hands," David said.

"She's the one who took the law into her own hands," Herman said, pointing at Jessie. "She

95

tried to make me think I was allergic to roses too. If that isn't against the law, it ought to be."

"I'm sorry about that, Herman," Jessie said. "I have a feeling I'm about to be very sorry for a lot of other things too."

"It's Simba, isn't it?" David asked, looking at the cat lying in Jessie's mother's arms. "You brought her all the way from Toronto?"

Jessie nodded as Simba jumped from Mrs. Bradley's arms to the floor. She walked to David and began to nudge against his ankles.

"Come on, Simba," Jessie said softly. "Come to me."

If Simba heard her, she had decided not to pay attention. At that moment she was too engrossed in David's ankles to notice anyone else, even Jessie.

"You've all caught me red-handed," Jessie said. "I smuggled her here and I've kept her hidden in my room."

"So this is the secret wedding present you've been working on in your room," David said, looking like he was about to get very mad at Jessie and Simba. He tried to shake Simba from his ankles. Simba didn't get the message. Finally, David picked her up. Before he could toss her away, his eyes met Simba's. She licked the back of his hand.

"I'm guilty," Jessie said. "I don't have any defense. Even if the Hijinxers hadn't suggested it, I would have brought her anyway. I just couldn't leave her behind. And there wasn't any way I could tell you the truth either."

"We'll have to report it to Carlos's father," Herman said. "Mr. Rodriguez will take care of the details. Right, Mr. Bradley?"

David didn't answer. He was too busy cuddling Simba. "I never had a cat before," he was saying to Jessie's mother. "She's beautiful, isn't she?"

"Cats are against the law at the Tudor Towers," Herman said. "Everyone knows that, Mr. Bradley."

"Rules can be changed," David said. "We could make up a petition and take it around. You boys would give us a week, wouldn't you?"

Before Carlos or Herman could say anything, Jessie spoke. "You're not mad at me, David?" she asked.

"I should be," he said. "But I'm not. Lawyers call it extenuating circumstances."

"What's that mean?" Carlos asked.

"It doesn't make what Jessie did right," David said. "But it means we understand why she did it. Anyone who ever saw Simba would understand." He stroked Simba. "Hi, Simba," he said.

"I'd like to take the petition around," Carlos said. "If it's okay with you, Jessie."

97

"And if we get it signed by a majority of the tenants, Simba gets to be legal?" Jessie asked.

"Could be," David said.

Jessie felt so happy that she was about to cry. Before she did, David gave her a handkerchief with his free hand.

"Do you have another one of those, Mr. Bradley?" Herman asked. Although he had momentarily stopped sneezing, his eyes were as red and teary as Jessie's.

"He's allergic to cats," Carlos explained.

"I sneeze because I'm allergic," Herman said as he wiped his eyes. "I cry when I get emotional."

"You're emotional now?" Carlos asked.

"I'm glad the cat's going to get a second chance," Herman said. "Even if I can't stand them, I still have feelings."

At that moment, everyone in apartment 14F was feeling as emotional as Herman. There was no way that any one of them could have suspected what danger Simba was in.

Chapter 13

3:14 P.M., SUNDAY

We, the undersigned, declare that:
1. This is a democracy.
2. In a democracy there should be no discrimination.
3. Dogs and cats should have equal rights.
4. Equal rights include housing.
5. Any tenant in the Tudor Towers should be allowed to keep any well-trained, well-behaved pet.

"Hey, Jessie, this is some petition your father wrote for us," Carlos said.

"Stepfather," Jessie said. "But close enough. David was also the first one to sign it. Once he fell in love with Simba, it was only a matter of time till he agreed to help us. I should have known that all along, I guess."

It was after lunch and Jessie and Carlos had

met in the lobby of the Tudor Towers, just as they had planned.

"Did you tell *your* father about the petition?" Jessie asked.

"Oh, sure," Carlos said. "He thinks it's okay just as long as we keep it democratic."

"Was he suspicious?"

"He's got too much on his mind to worry about illegal pets in the Tudor Towers," Carlos said. "Some of the tenants are beginning to blame him for the cat burglar."

"But that's not fair," Jessie said. "Even the police haven't been able to do anything."

"Try explaining that to Colonel Wendell," Carlos said. "He says if the cat burglar isn't caught and caught soon, my dad is going to get the ax."

"They're going to fire him?" Jessie asked. "Can they do that?"

"If enough people agree with the colonel, they can," Carlos said sadly. "And my dad will have to get another job someplace else."

"And you'll have to live someplace else too," Jessie said just as sadly. "If someone finds out about Simba before we get the petition signed, maybe they'll make my family leave too."

"Well, I'm glad to do what I can to make sure that doesn't happen, Jessie."

"I want to help find the cat burglar," Jessie

said. "I don't want your family to leave the Tudor Towers either."

"There's not much we can do, Jessie," Carlos said. "My father's doing everything he can."

"I've had experience with this sort of thing," Jessie said. "Maybe I'll come up with something."

"You've caught criminals?"

"Not exactly," Jessie admitted. "But back in Toronto I was a member of the Hijinx Club. We pulled off a whole lot of stunts. You'd be surprised how much I learned from the experience. I bet I can apply some of my know-how to the cat burglar case."

"But the police can't crack the case," Carlos said. "There are guards here every night and they've never seen anyone suspicious going in or going out of the Tudor Towers the nights that cat burglar strikes."

"Maybe the cat burglar isn't suspicious-looking," Jessie said. "Have the police thought of that possibility?"

"Of course they have," Carlos said. "But they take down the names of everyone they see and so far everyone has been a tenant of the Tudor Towers or a guest of one of the tenants."

"They're sure?"

"Everything checks out."

103

"I'll come up with something," Jessie said. "I always do."

"While you're thinking up the solution to the crimes around here, I think we ought to get this petition going."

"You're right," Jessie said. "Who should we take it to first?"

"Someone easy," Carlos said.

"You mean someone nice? Someone who would be sure to sign it?"

"Yeah."

"Yeah. I know who!" Jessie said. "Mr. and Mrs. Smith-Jones!"

"Do they like dogs and cats?"

"Well, I never discussed it with them," Jessie said, "but they're so nice I bet they do."

"And they're very popular around here," Carlos said. "If the other tenants see they've signed the petition, they'll sign it too."

It was Mrs. Smith-Jones who opened the door. She was delighted to see them. She led them onto the terrace, where her husband was reading *The Miami Herald.* He, too, was delighted to see them.

Carlos gave him the petition.

"Will you please read that, sir?"

Mr. Smith-Jones read it aloud. He read in a deep, solemn voice that made the petition sound very, very important. Almost like the Gettysburg Address or the Declaration of Independence. When he finished, Mrs. Smith-Jones applauded. And her husband echoed her sentiments.

"Bravo!" he rumbled. "Bravo!"

"Then you'll both sign?" Carlos asked.

"Of course," they both said.

"I just knew you liked pets," Jessie said.

"That's an understatement," Mrs. Smith-Jones said. "Especially when it comes to Sydney and cats."

"Yes, I love them," Mr. Smith-Jones said. "I long to have one for my very own."

"Well, if the petition goes through, you'll be able to," Jessie said.

"I don't know how I'll wait that long," he said. Then he chuckled. Then he laughed so hard that he started coughing. Mrs. Smith-Jones pounded him on the back. Carlos and Jessie couldn't see what was all that funny, but Mr. and Mrs. Smith-Jones both signed the petition and that was all that mattered. The petition was off to a good start.

Then Mrs. Amos, 17D, signed the petition.

So did Mr. and Mrs. Jeffers, 16E.

And then Miss Martholomew, 16A, signed it.

It was too good to be true, they thought. It couldn't last. And sure enough they were right. It didn't.

When they knocked on the door of 15C, Colonel Wendell answered it. He looked at the two of them and said, "Yes, what is it?" He didn't ask them in.

"Will you please read this, sir?" Carlos asked.

The colonel read the petition.

Then the colonel blew his top.

"What is this building coming to? It's a disgrace! That's what it is. A downright disgrace. Burglars all over the place. No one safe and nothing being done about it. And now this! A petition to allow cats and dogs in the Tudor Towers. No, sir, I will have none of that. You can be certain I will fight it tooth and nail. The day will never come when animals are allowed in my building. Over my dead body!"

The colonel closed the door firmly in Carlos and Jessie's faces. They were shaken, almost frightened by Colonel Wendell's anger. But then Jessie thought of Simba and of life without Simba. And that gave her the courage to give Carlos the courage to carry on.

"The colonel," Jessie sighed. "Is he always so mean?"

"Most of the time he is," Carlos said.

"I wish he were the cat burglar," Jessie said. "Then they'd arrest him and take him away."

"The colonel is the most law-abiding man in the Tudor Towers," Carlos said.

106

"But he could come in and out without arousing suspicion," Jessie said. "It's a possibility, isn't it?"

"Anyone who lives here can come and go without seeming suspicious to the guards," Carlos said.

"So anyone who lives here could be a suspect," Jessie said.

"It's not very likely," Carlos said. "People here are pretty well off. No one has a reason to steal."

"Yeah," Jessie sighed. "I see what you mean. Still . . ."

After their visit to the colonel their luck seemed to change. When it was time for them to go home to dinner, they added up the score. It was discouraging. Lots more people refused to sign the petition than signed it. Well, tomorrow was another day. Maybe their luck would change again—this time for the better.

They said good-bye to each other in the lobby. As Jessie pushed her floor in the elevator, she thought about the cat burglar. Carlos was right, she decided. No one who lived in the Tudor Towers made a very good suspect. Not even Colonel Wendell, she had to admit. As much as she wanted to help catch the cat burglar and keep Carlos's father from losing his job, she knew she had better stick with her petition and Simba. Her cat and the cat burglar had nothing to do with each other. You didn't have to be a genius to know that.

Chapter 14

9:43 P.M., SUNDAY

That night the cat burglar struck again.

The target was the Lomasks, the richest tenants in the Tudor Towers. As Mr. and Mrs. Smith-Jones had hoped, their haul was the greatest of their long, lucrative, and infamous career. When they walked away from apartment 9D, their pockets and their shopping bags were bulging with loot. Thin, little Mrs. Smith-Jones looked almost as stout as her husband. Over her cat burglar getup and under her long cloak, she was wearing Mrs. Lomask's mink, her sable, and her ermine.

Back in their own apartment, over tea and biscuits, Mr. and Mrs. Smith-Jones gloated over the night's take. Besides the furs there was all the jewelry that Mrs. Lomask had not worn this night to the concert in Palm Beach. Rings and pins, earrings and bracelets, diamonds, pearls, rubies, and emeralds. There were assorted watches, some jeweled, all either gold or platinum. There were priceless candlesticks, silverware, and a coffee service. There was almost a thousand dollars in cash, almost ten thousand in bonds.

"Well, my dear," Mrs. Smith-Jones said, beaming. "Was it worth waiting a bit longer for that cat you want?"

"Financially, yes," Mr. Smith-Jones said, "but if I had to choose between all this and that divine cat . . ."

"You would choose the cat?"

"Without hesitation," Mr. Smith-Jones said. "I would choose the cat."

"My dear, I am becoming quite jealous of your cat," Mrs. Smith-Jones said.

"Nonsense, my dear."

"Well, at any rate, this time tomorrow night the cat will be all yours, Sydney."

"All mine," Mr. Smith-Jones sighed.

"We know that Mr. and Mrs. Bradley will be out tomorrow night," Mrs. Smith-Jones said. "But we'll have to do something about getting rid of Jessica. We don't want anyone in the apartment waiting for us except that cat."

"My cat," Mr. Smith-Jones said.

"Then we go to South America," Mrs. Smith-Jones said.

"Olé!" Mr. Smith-Jones said.

And then they both giggled.

It was noon the next day, Monday, when once again the colonel was standing in Mr. Rodriguez's office and once again he was shouting at Mr. Rodriguez. "And last night the Lomasks' apartment was ransacked by the cat burglar. Ransacked, sir. Cleaned out. Is there no end to this outrage?" he bellowed.

"Colonel," Mr. Rodriguez said. "I am doing everything possible."

"Not good enough, hardly good enough!" the colonel shouted. "I suggest you try doing the impossible!"

"And what would that be?" Mr. Rodriguez asked.

"That is for you to find out," the colonel said coldly. "You're the manager here."

"But, Colonel, if the police can't track down the cat burglar . . ."

"Forget the police! It's your responsibility, sir. If the cat burglar is not apprehended in the next twenty-four hours, and all the stolen property returned to their rightful owners, your head will roll!"

"Is that a threat, Colonel?"

"No, it's an ultimatum," the colonel said. "Tonight we're having a tenants' meeting in the

111

lobby. You will see that I'm not alone. If you don't catch the cat burglar, you will be fired."

Mr. Rodriguez sank into the chair behind his desk.

Well, he thought, it was a fine job while it lasted. He had no idea where he would find another job. That wasn't so easy nowadays. And if he did find another job, it probably wouldn't be in Florida. Jobs in Florida were prime jobs. His wife and his son would hate having to leave. They both loved Florida. So did he.

Mr. Rodriguez sighed hopelessly.

How was it possible to do the impossible?

In twenty-four hours?

That afternoon, after school, Carlos and Jessie picked up where they had left off the day before and took their petition through the next three floors. At five o'clock they added up the score.

It was discouraging again. A lot of tenants, Carlos and Jessie were beginning to understand, had bought condos here because of the no-pet rule.

"But I'm not giving up!" Jessie said.

"Me neither," Carlos said.

"Tomorrow's another day!"

"Every tomorrow is!"

They shook hands on that, but Jessie was seriously worried.

It had been a busy day for the Smith-Joneses. All their clothes were packed and stowed in their station wagon in the basement garage, ready for their getaway. The things they had stolen, jewels and watches and silver and gold, were too valuable to leave unguarded in their car, so it was all in their apartment, packed in innocent-looking shopping bags, ready to go with them. Mrs. Smith-Jones hummed as she checked her uniform. When she got to South America, she would have Mr. Rodriguez sell the condo and send them the money.

She looked at the clock.

It was nearly five-thirty. Time to make her phone calls. As she dialed the first number, Mr. Smith-Jones came into the living room. He sat down on the couch to listen to his wife.

"Hello, Jessica," she said. She didn't sound at all like herself. Her accent wasn't British. It was American with a slight Cuban accent. "This is Mrs. Rodriguez. Carlos's mother. There's to be a tenants' meeting in the lobby tonight. Carlos just found out and has been trying to reach you. He thinks you could get more signatures for your petition there. He had to go out for a while, so he asked me to ask you."

Mrs. Smith-Jones waited a moment and then said, "You will. Well, that's just fine. Better make

113

that eight-thirty sharp. Carlos will be waiting for you in the lobby."

She hung up and looked at her husband. He smiled.

"You are a very clever one, my dear," he said admiringly.

Mrs. Smith-Jones dialed another number.

"Hello," she said. "May I speak with Carlos Rodriguez please? Thank you." Now her accent was completely American. "This is Mrs. Bradley, Jessie's mother. Jessie has been trying to reach you. She thinks you can get some more signatures at the tenants' meeting tonight. She had to go out. Otherwise she would have asked you herself."

After another moment, she hung up and smiled at her husband.

"Thank you, Milly," he said. "You've made me the happiest cat burglar in the world."

"Least I could do. Soon we won't be cat burglars."

They smiled lovingly at each other.

Chapter 15

8:23 P.M., MONDAY

Jessie got to the lobby a little early but Carlos was already there waiting for her. She had some good news she wanted to share with him.

"My mom got us a couple more votes," she said.

"How come?"

"She went for a sunset sail with the Cowens
. . ."

"3F," Carlos said.

"Mom told them about our petition and they're not anticat and dog. They'll both sign tomorrow."

"Every little bit helps," Carlos said.

Jessica took one copy of the petition and stood by the elevator. Carlos stood by the other elevator with another copy of the petition. They were all set to go to work for Simba, but something was bothering Carlos.

"Did you say your mother went for a sunset sail?" he asked.

"Yes, with the Cowens," Jessie said.

"How long was she gone?"

"Oh, more than an hour. Why?"

"Like from five to six?" Carlos asked.

"Like from five to six-thirty," Jessie said. "Why?"

"Do the Cowens have a telephone on their boat?" Carlos asked.

"No, of course not," Jessie said. "It's just a little boat."

"Then how could your mother have called me at five-thirty?" Carlos asked.

"My mother phoned you?" Jessie asked.

"About the tenants' meeting," Carlos said.

"My mother didn't phone you," Jessie said. "Your mother phoned me."

"No," Carlos said. "Your mother phoned me."

Jessie just stared at Carlos.

"Someone wanted us out of our apartments tonight," Carlos said.

"The cat burglar," Jessie said anxiously.

"That can't be it," Carlos said. "My mother's at home. The cat burglar never robs anyone while there are people at home."

"But Mom and David went to a dinner party," Jessie said. "Our apartment is empty except for Simba."

"Well, at least you don't have to worry about her," Carlos said.

Jessie bit her lip. "I *am* worried about Simba, Carlos," she said. "She's in danger. I can feel it. Somebody's up to something, Carlos, and it's somebody who knows both of us."

"But who, Jessie?"

"The cat burglar," Jessie said. "We were wrong, Carlos. The cat burglar has to be someone who lives in the Tudor Towers."

"But Simba's not in danger," Carlos said. "Cat burglars don't steal cats."

"Simba is the most precious thing in our apartment," Jessie cried. "Come on. We've got to get to the apartment before the cat burglar does."

Before Carlos could say another word, Jessie slammed her hand against the elevator button.

In the dark of the night Mrs. Smith-Jones swung happily from balcony to balcony. The ex-trapeze artist had never enjoyed her work more. First, as a young woman, she had done it to earn a living. Then she had done it to steal money and jewels. Tonight she was doing it for her husband.

She landed on the balcony of 14F.

The terrace door was unlocked. She had seen to that earlier by calling on Mrs. Bradley to borrow a cup of sugar. While Jessie's mother had been in the kitchen pouring the sugar, Mrs. Smith-Jones had unlocked the terrace door.

Now she closed the terrace door behind her and went to the front door. When she heard the three sharp raps, she let her prompt and portly husband into the apartment. He was carrying three large shopping bags filled with loot, their harvest from their stay at the Tudor Towers. As soon as they had stolen the cat, they would go directly to their getaway car in the garage in the basement. Now they went straight to Jessie's bedroom. Mr. Smith-Jones followed the pencil-thin beam of his flashlight.

"Here, kitty, kitty, kitty," he called gently.

Simba was sound asleep on Jessie's bed. When she woke, she thought that Jessie had come home. She sat up. Then she saw it wasn't Jessie at all. It was the same two people who had awakened her from her sleep two nights before. She didn't like them any better now than she did then.

Mr. Smith-Jones tried to make friends with her. He petted her and said flattering things. But Simba wasn't taken in. She bared her teeth and glared and hissed.

"Just as I thought, my dear," Mrs. Smith-Jones said. "We must take drastic means."

"Yes, I can see we must."

Mr. Smith-Jones handed the flashlight to his

wife and reached for the cat. Simba struggled but it was no use. Two big human hands were putting her into a burlap bag.

They walked from Jessie's room toward the front door. Just as Mr. Smith-Jones reached for the door, the doorbell rang.

Mr. and Mrs. Smith-Jones froze, listening and waiting.

Herman Riley rang the doorbell again.

He hoped that Jessie or her parents were home. Herman was in trouble. A book he had taken from the library was overdue. He had looked everywhere in the apartment for it and couldn't find it anywhere. His father was very annoyed with him. It wasn't just the fine that bothered Herman's father. He thought that if a boy couldn't get a book back to the library on time, he probably shouldn't be going to any Dolphin games at all.

Herman rang the doorbell a third time.

He remembered he had been reading the book when Carlos had come to his apartment. Herman sort of remembered taking it with him when they had sold magazine subscriptions. He hoped that he had left it in the Bradleys' apartment.

Heck, Herman thought, there's no one home.

119

He rang once more. Just in case. He waited another minute, but no one came to the door.

Well, they'll be back later, he thought. Herman gave up and went away.

Mrs. Smith-Jones, her ear pressed against the inside of the door, heard footsteps going down the corridor. She opened the door and listened some more. When she heard the elevator door open and close, she looked cautiously down the hall.

No one was in sight.

She and Mr. Smith-Jones crept quickly into the corridor.

They didn't dare take the elevator; one of the other tenants might be on it, and Simba might suddenly start to make a lot of noise.

So they used the fire stairs.

They started down the twenty flights of steps to their station wagon in the basement garage. Mr. Smith-Jones almost laughed with joy. In a few minutes they would be on their way to South America.

With the most darling cat in the world.

Chapter 16

8:36 P.M., MONDAY

The elevator indicator said the nearer elevator was at the fourteenth floor when Carlos pushed the button. It started to descend. It's moving so slowly, Jessie thought. It had never come down this slowly before.

They checked the other elevator. It was on the nineteenth floor. Even worse. So they went back to the first elevator. Eleven . . . ten . . . nine . . . eight . . . Oh, don't let the cat burglar get Simba, she prayed. I promise I'll never leave her again. . . . Four . . . three . . . two. And then at last the doors opened and Carlos and Jessie jumped in.

It seemed to Jessie that the elevator was going up even more slowly than it had come down. She closed her eyes and prayed some more. She thought that she could have run up the stairs faster. Then the elevator stopped at her floor and they were racing down the long corridor.

At 14F Carlos took the key out of Jessie's trembling hand and unlocked the door.

There was a lamp burning in the living room; to Carlos the room looked undisturbed, everything in its proper place. While he looked in the master bedroom, Jessie went into her room calling for Simba. The master bedroom also looked neat and tidy, not as though any burglar had been ransacking it. Carlos guessed they had got there before the cat burglar did. He went back to the living room.

Jessie was coming out of the bedroom. Her face was white and she looked dreadful.

"Jessie," he said, "what's wrong?"

"Simba," she said. "She's gone. The cat burglar stole her."

"No," Carlos said. "The cat burglar wouldn't do that. Simba's got to be here somewhere."

"No," Jessie said. "Simba always comes running the moment I call her. No matter where she is, she always comes."

Even though Carlos wasn't sure that Simba had been stolen, he helped Jessie hunt for the cat. They looked in the kitchen and the dining room and in all the closets and cupboards and even under the sofa and the chairs, just in case Simba had fallen asleep under one of them.

Carlos had to admit that Simba was gone.

"We'll call the police," he said. "They'll find her."

"The police!" Jessie said hopelessly. "All this time they couldn't catch the cat burglar. How can they catch him now?"

"But we've got to do something," Carlos said.

"Like what?"

"I don't know," Carlos said. He felt as helpless as Jessie felt hopeless.

Just then they heard a sound behind them. A great big noisy sneeze. They turned. Herman was standing in the doorway.

"Hey, Jessie," he said. "Do you know if I left my library book here?"

Carlos and Jessie had only to look at each other. They didn't have to say out loud what they were both thinking.

"Herman," Jessie began.

"I'm not coming in," Herman said. "On account of I'm allergic. I just want to know if my library book was . . ."

"Simba's been stolen," Jessie said.

"By the cat burglar," Carlos said.

"You're our only hope," Jessie pleaded.

"Well," Herman said.

"Please, Herman."

Herman knew what they wanted, but he knew it would mean a lot of sneezing. He looked at

123

Jessie. She looked as if her world had come to an end.

"Get me a box of Kleenex," he said. "What are we waiting for?"

They followed Herman out into the hall. He turned right, toward the elevator, but after a few steps he stopped. He took a deep breath and waited.

He didn't sneeze.

"No," Herman said. "Your cat didn't come this way."

So they turned around and went back, on past the door to 14F. A few steps past it, Herman began sneezing.

"This is the way," he said. "Come on!"

They followed Herman all the way to the end of the hall, where the fire door was. They pushed open the door and went through onto the landing. Herman gave another great sneeze.

"Your cat went this way," he said. "Follow me!"

They chased Herman down the flights of stairs, running as fast as they could. Herman was sneezing regularly now, practically one sneeze a flight. He and Jessie and Carlos knew they must be hot on the trail. They knew they were getting nearer and nearer to Simba.

They went past the lobby floor. They were on the steps of the basement.

124

"The garage," Carlos shouted. "The cat burglar must be making his getaway in a car."

Herman didn't say anything. He was sneezing too hard.

Then they were in the garage.

A big station wagon was moving out of its parking space.

"Stop, thief!" Carlos cried.

"Stop, thief!" Jessie cried.

Herman sneezed some more.

But the car didn't stop or even slow down. It went faster. It moved through the light beam that controlled the garage doors. The door began to roll up.

Carlos wheeled around and lunged for the fuse box on the wall. He opened it and unscrewed the fuse. The garage doors stopped just where they were. And the lights went out. Jessie and Carlos and Herman were standing in the pitch dark with the cat burglar.

For a long moment it was absolutely silent. Then they heard a car door open and close. They heard footsteps moving away from them. They followed the sound of the footsteps, stumbling and bumping into things, through the dark laundry and the storage room, then up the fire escape stairway to the first floor. They saw the fire door settling back into its frame.

"The parking lot!" Carlos yelled. "C'mon!"

They raced through the lobby and passed the colonel and Tom, the night doorman, who were standing at the entrance.

The lights in the parking lot were on and made it as bright as day. Jessie stopped dead in her tracks, staring in amazement and disbelief.

The people they were chasing were the Smith-Joneses.

Jessie couldn't believe that Mr. and Mrs. Smith-Jones were crooks. She knew they would never, never try to steal Simba. But there they were, their arms filled with shopping bags. And one burlap bag. They were running from car to car until they found one with keys in the ignition. Jessie saw that it was Colonel Wendell's Cadillac. The Smith-Joneses started to get into it, but when they heard Jessie and Carlos and Herman running toward them, still shouting "Stop, thief!" they turned. Then Mr. Smith-Jones dropped one of the shopping bags. It broke on the pavement and Mrs. Smith-Jones knelt to scoop up jewels that had fallen from the bag.

"Stand back!" Mr. Smith-Jones yelled. His voice was not nice and cheerful now. It was mean and nasty. "Don't anyone move one step!" Then he said to his wife, "Get in the car, my dear. You do the driving."

Mrs. Smith-Jones opened the car door and swung the bag over the back of the front seat

127

and dropped it on the floor there. Then she got behind the wheel and started the motor.

Simba didn't know where she was. She only knew that she was closed up in some dreadful bag and for the last few minutes had been bounced around, up and down and sideways, until her head was spinning. Now the bouncing had stopped. She shook her head to clear it.

She heard Jessie's voice, shouting louder than she had ever heard her shout before. Simba found her way out of the burlap bag. She was still dazed, but she knew she was in a car. She jumped on the back of the seat so she could see better.

In the front seat she saw the strange woman who had twice wakened her from a sound sleep. Outside was the strange man she hated.

The blood of her Siamese ancestors pulsed through her veins. She crawled out the window and up onto the roof of the car. She poised herself. She leaped from the car roof onto Jessie's shoulder.

Then she leaped at Mr. Smith-Jones. She landed on his arm and dug her teeth and claws into his right wrist. Her claws dug deeper into his flesh. Mr. Smith-Jones screamed in agony and fell to the ground. Then Colonel Wendell and Tom the doorman were running toward him.

There was shouting and yelling, but the next thing Simba knew, she was in Jessie's arms and Jessie was laughing and crying.

And giving Simba's back a good stroking.

Chapter 17

11:41 A.M., SATURDAY, ONE MONTH LATER

Jessie was happily stretched out in a deck chair beside the Tudor Towers swimming pool watching Carlos practice the Australian crawl. At her feet Simba was curled up for all the world to see. She was no longer an illegal cat.

What had happened the day after Simba had caught Mr. and Mrs. Smith-Jones practically single-handedly was like a dream come true. Jessie and Carlos didn't have to take their petition around again. The people came to them. They came in droves, falling over each other, to sign the petition in favor of cats and dogs. It was a landslide.

Carlos climbed out of the pool and came to sit beside Jessie. Simba jumped from Jessie's feet onto Carlos's lap and asked to be stroked between the eyes. He had been spending so much time with Jessie lately that Simba had taught him all her signals.

A collie puppy on the other side of the pool woke up and saw an empty lap. He crawled out from under a deck chair and made himself comfortable on Jessie's lap. Jessie patted him on the head.

Just then, Mr. and Mrs. Cowen, 3F, came along with their sheep dog, Gilda, on her leash. They stopped to say hello to Jessie and Carlos.

"How does Gilda like living in the Tudor Towers?" Jessie asked.

"Gilda couldn't be happier," Mr. Cowen said. "Thanks to Simba."

"Yes," Mrs. Cowen said. "How is the little mother today?"

"She's feeling very proud of herself," Jessie said. "Aren't you, Simba?"

Two days after it was legal for cats to live in the Tudor Towers, Simba, to everyone's surprise, had given birth to seven babies. Seven Siamese kittens, all the spitting image of their mother.

Jessie had given away all but two of Simba's kittens. But all five of them were close by, right in the Tudor Towers. Simba was able to keep checking on all her children every day to make sure that they were being properly brought up. So far, all of them were.

As Mr. and Mrs. Cowen walked on with Gilda, they passed Mr. and Mrs. Lomask, who were exercising their Great Dane. The Cowens and the Lomasks said hello to one another. Gilda and Thor had only a nodding acquaintance so they only nodded to each other.

Now Herman came racing out to the pool. He was so breathless with excitement that he had to sit down for a minute to catch his breath. Simba jumped from Carlos's lap onto Herman's.

"Did you hear the news?" Herman asked them. "It was just on the radio!"

"What news?" Jessie asked.

"About Mr. and Mrs. Smith-Jones," Herman said.

"No," Jessie said. "What is it?"

"They were found guilty of grand larceny," Herman said.

"How about," Jessie asked, "attempted catnapping?"

Herman didn't answer Jessie. He had stopped listening and was staring down at his lap. "Hey, hey, look at that."

"We're looking!" Carlos and Jessie said.

"I've got a cat on my lap," Herman said. "I've got a cat sitting right on me."

133

"Yes, we noticed that," Carlos said.

"But I'm not sneezing," Herman said. "I feel fine. What happened to my allergy?"

"Maybe your doctor was right," Carlos said. "Maybe all the glory you got from the Incredible Cat Caper pushed the allergy out."

"You don't sound like a specialist," Herman said. "But my allergy is definitely, positively gone."

"Herman," Jessie said. "Simba still has two kittens. Would you like to have one?"

"You mean you'll give me one?"

"It would be a pleasure."

"But I couldn't do that to Simba," Herman said. "I couldn't take one of her last two kittens."

"You deserve one," Carlos said. "If it hadn't been for you, the Smith-Joneses would be in South America now instead of jail."

"If it hadn't been for Simba," Herman said, "they might have got away."

"You saved Simba too," Jessie said. "I know she would like you to have one of her kittens."

"Holy cow!" Herman yelled. "I've got a cat of my own. My mother and dad will be so proud of me."

"I've got an extra piece of good news," Jessie said. "The Hijinxers are going international. My friends in Toronto think it's great if we start a branch in the United States."

"And we're all going to be full-fledged members?" Carlos asked.

"Of course we are," Jessie said.

"Even me?" Herman asked.

"Especially you," Jessie said. "And Simba. She's the official mascot, of course."

Then a military figure came marching up and halted beside them. There was a tiny kitten perched on his shoulder. The kitten was the spitting image of Simba.

"Good morning, everybody," Colonel Wendell boomed. "How are you all?"

They all said they were fine.

"Have you named your kitten yet, Colonel?" Jessie asked.

"Yes, I have," said the Colonel. "I've named it after its brave and gallant mother."

"But it's a boy," Herman said.

"I'm calling him Simbo," the Colonel said. "That's the masculine of Simba. Don't know how I ever got along without a cat. Perched on my shoulder. Ready to spring against my enemies. Never felt so safe in all my days. Well, must be cracking now. Nice seeing you all!"

"Good-bye, Colonel," Carlos and Jessie and Herman said.

"Good-bye, everybody!"

Herman stroked the back of Simba's neck. "I don't know how I got along without a cat either, but even so, I think I got enough excitement from the caper to last me a while."

Jessie smiled, but she didn't tell Herman that she had a sneaky feeling there would be more adventures ahead for all three of them.

About the Authors

KELLEY ROOS is the pen name for the Edgar Award–winning writers, Audrey Kelley Roos and William Roos, Stephen Roos's parents. Mr. Roos lives on Martha's Vineyard, Massachusetts.

STEPHEN ROOS is the author of *My Horrible Secret, The Terrible Truth,* and *My Secret Admirer,* all available in Delacorte Press and Dell Yearling editions. He divides his time between Ulster County, New York and Key West, Florida.

About the Illustrator

KATHERINE COVILLE illustrated *The Skull in the Snow* by Toni McCarthy, published by Delacorte Press. She lives in Fulton, New York.